"I have you right where I want you..."

Rick smiled as he said the words and wrapped his arms around her. He hugged Lindsey so tightly that she actually felt a bit light-headed.

"I can't seem to keep my hands off you."

"I noticed."

"Or my mouth." He nuzzled the side of her neck, then pressed light kisses across her collarbone.

She shuddered, and slowly, deliberately, moved her hips against his. Her entire body tingled with awareness. She couldn't believe their chemistry was still this strong after six years of not seeing each other. It was almost embarrassing.

"Let's order room service," he said. "We'll eat on the balcony. Share a nice bottle of wine. Remember?"

Oh, she remembered all right. The cool air danced across her skin, making her shiver. Or maybe it was the way he stared at her, his eyes dark with promise and danger, as if his plans for her landed on the other side of wicked. The thought triggered a delicious tingle of anticipation.

"Perfect," she whispered into his ear and kissed him gently once, twice on his cheek. "You're perfect."

Blaze™

Dear Reader,

When I was a teenager living in Hawaii, surfing was big. You didn't have to watch the news or listen to the radio to know when the swells were up. Half an empty classroom said it all. I never thought about it then, but looking back now, I don't think many people considered ditching school to go surfing was the same as cutting class. If they did, the beaches would have been crawling with truant officers instead of sand crabs. Surfing was simply part of the culture. That said, because I attended a small private school until my senior year, absences were not tolerated and yours truly was stuck at a desk sweating over Algebra.

Still, that didn't keep me from the surfing beaches. Because there were boys there. Really cute boys with killer bodies. That was high school, though, and my tastes have vastly changed since then.

I never thought I'd write a surfer hero. But when it came time to create a second story for my Spring Break series, Rick Granger wiggled his way into my brain and stuck. He was perfect for shy, sheltered Lindsey. Who better to convince her that she already was the strong woman she wanted to become? The kind of woman who ended up helping Rick put his own life into perspective.

I very much enjoyed crafting both characters. I hope you enjoy them, too, as well as a glimpse of the quieter side of Hawaii.

Best wishes,

Debbi Rawlins

Debbi Rawlins

DELICIOUS DO-OVER

TORONTO NEW YORK LONDON
AMSTERDAM PARIS SYDNEY HAMBURG
STOCKHOLM ATHENS TOKYO MILAN MADRID
PRAGUE WARSAW BUDAPEST AUCKLAND

Recycling programs
for this product may
not exist in your area.

ISBN-13: 978-0-373-79613-7

DELICIOUS DO-OVER

ABOUT THE AUTHOR

Debbi Rawlins lives in central Utah, out in the country, surrounded by woods and deer and wild turkeys. It's quite a change for a city girl who didn't even know where the state of Utah was until four years ago. Of course, unfamiliarity has never stopped her. Between her junior and senior years of college she spontaneously left her home in Hawaii and bummed around Europe for five weeks by herself. And much to her parents' delight, returned home with only a quarter in her wallet.

Books by Debbi Rawlins

HARLEQUIN BLAZE

13—IN HIS WILDEST DREAMS
36—EDUCATING GINA
60—HANDS ON
112—ANYTHING GOES…
143—HE'S ALL THAT*
159—GOOD TO BE BAD
183—A GLIMPSE OF FIRE
220—HOT SPOT**
250—THE HONEYMOON THAT WASN'T
312—SLOW HAND LUKE
351—IF HE ONLY KNEW…*
368—WHAT SHE *REALLY* WANTS FOR CHRISTMAS†
417—ALL OR NOTHING
455—ONCE AN OUTLAW††
467—ONCE A REBEL††
491—TEXAS HEAT
509—TEXAS BLAZE
528—LONE STAR LOVER††
603—SECOND TIME LUCKY‡

*Men To Do
**Do Not Disturb
†Million Dollar Secrets
††Stolen from Time
‡Spring Break

Prologue

LINDSEY SHAW blinked when the champagne flute refused to come into focus. She couldn't be drunk, or even tipsy. Not after only two and a half glasses. But then she rarely drank alcohol, and hadn't eaten since the granola bar she'd forced down while on the plane this morning.

She looked over at her friend Mia and then her other friend Shelby. They didn't look blurry. A bit flushed, happy, excited. She wished she shared her new business partners' optimism over the gigantic step they'd just taken. But the truth was, she was scared to death.

"Uh, Lindsey, you do know we're celebrating, right?" Grinning, Mia picked up the champagne bottle and started to refill glasses.

Lindsey quickly grabbed her half-empty flute. "No more for me until we eat something."

"Seriously?" Shelby made a face. "And ruin our buzz?"

"I'm not flying back to Chicago tomorrow morning with a hangover." Lindsey hadn't meant to sound defensive. Now wasn't the time to get squeamish. She'd agreed to take the plunge. Sign her life away. Give up her job. Move back to Manhattan. She wouldn't change her mind now. Even though she wanted to throw up just thinking about the uncertainty they faced in starting the new business.

"Sometimes you're just no fun."

"Shut up, Shelby." Mia set the bottle back in the silver bucket. "This is huge. Not that I don't have total faith in us, but let's be real. We are taking a big risk."

Lindsey's stomach clenched. The three of them had talked about opening the concierge/rental business ever since junior year in college, when their sorority had used the concept for a fundraiser. Then they had only rented themselves out, but the new business would be more comprehensive, renting out everything from designer purses and iPhones, to college students willing to run errands or host parties. It was a perfect concept for a city like Manhattan, and in theory she'd been all for it, until it meant giving up everything that made her feel safe and secure.

Mia happily lifted her refilled flute. "To Anything Goes."

"I think we've already made that toast." Shelby grinned and clinked her glass to Mia's.

"A couple of times," Lindsey murmured, then smiled gamely and raised her glass in solidarity.

These were her best friends in the whole world. She'd missed them desperately since moving to Chicago after graduation. It hadn't been enough that they talked or texted every day, or that they got together twice a year. They were all busy with their jobs, and life seemed to be passing them by.

Mia had been the one gutsy enough to do something about it. She'd made the call, got them all on a conference line and reminded them that they'd sworn on their beloved iPods that once they'd saved enough money, they would take the leap. Lindsey admired Mia's confidence and take-charge personality. And Shelby was just so charming and comfortable in her own skin that Lindsey was unashamedly envious. If she were going to gamble her future on anyone, it would be these two.

Not *if*. She'd already signed the loan documents. Two hours ago. Mia would turn in her resignation tomorrow. Shelby would submit hers when she returned to Houston on Monday. Lindsey had to step up and do the same.

She stared out the bar's window at the gathering darkness, squinting when she thought she saw snow flurries. Certainly not impossible. It was early March after all.

Blinking, she heard a couple of key words that made her realize she'd missed out on part of the conversation. The discussion had turned to men, or the lack thereof.

"It's not like when we were in college," Mia was saying. "Manhattan isn't exactly teeming with eligible men."

"Well, neither is Chicago," Lindsey added. "I haven't had a real date in seven months." She eyed Shelby, who never seemed to have trouble in that department. "Maybe we should've moved to Houston, Mia. If things got too bad, at least we could count on leftovers."

Shelby waved a hand. "Oh, sweetie, you're delusional if you think I've had any better luck there."

Lindsey snorted. "Right."

Mia's brows arched. "Really, Shelby?"

"Really," she answered defensively, and then shrugged.

"I can't remember the last time I went out a second or third time with the same guy and those are the dates that count." She sniffed. "And no, it's not because I'm too picky."

"You have every reason to be damn picky. We all do," Mia said.

"Amen." Lindsey downed a sip, even after she'd told herself to lay off for a while. "Still would be nice to have an assortment to be picky over." She frowned at Mia. "Whatever happened to that guy you worked with? David, right?"

Mia choked out a laugh. "There was never anything there."

"Yeah, I remember him," Shelby said. "When you first started with the firm you thought he was hot."

"He is hot. Sadly, he's taken."

"Married?" Lindsey said sympathetically. She'd nearly made that mistake with a guy who worked for the same accounting firm she did. Fortunately, he worked out of the Detroit office and their flirting had taken place over the phone. Good thing she'd found out the jerk was married before she'd met him in person.

"To the job," Mia said, and went on about David being too chicken to break company policy. Then she grabbed the champagne, and topped off everyone's glasses. "This is what I don't get…when we were in school there were all kinds of guys around. If we didn't have a date, it was because we didn't want to go out."

"I know, right?" Shelby frowned thoughtfully. "Even when we went out in groups, guys always outnumbered us. So what the hell happened to them? They can't *all* be married and living in the burbs."

"You have a point." Mia sipped slowly. "Even during spring break, I swear, there were two guys to every girl."

"I'm the accountant," Lindsey said. "I'd say more like three to one."

"Junior year. Fort Lauderdale." Shelby slumped back, sighing. "Oh, my God."

"Are you kidding?" Mia stared at her in disbelief. "Come on. Senior year, Waikiki beach, hands-down winner."

Lindsey smiled broadly. "Yep," she said, easily recalling Rick's face. His body. Oh, God, what a night that had been.

"Hey, guys," Mia said, after a long silence. "I have an idea."

"Oh, no." Lindsey groaned. "I don't know if I can take another one."

"No, this is good." Mia grinned. "There's no law that says spring break is just for college kids."

"Okay." Shelby drew out the word.

Lindsey had the distinct feeling she wouldn't like where this conversation was headed.

"We're going to be working our asses off until we get Anything Goes off the ground, right? If we want to take a vacation, this is the time. Probably the last time for years. Who knows, maybe we'll even get laid."

Lindsey frowned. "Hawaii?"

"Why not?" Mia glanced at the empty champagne bottle and signaled the waiter.

"Because it's too expensive, for one thing. Are you forgetting we've just signed our lives away?"

"I don't know." Mia sighed, moved a shoulder.

"Maybe we can go on the cheap, pick up one of those last-minute deals."

"It wouldn't hurt to see what's available," Shelby said.

Lindsey hated the idea, but she figured she'd get voted off the island. "I suppose not." She set down her glass, her head spinning. "But we'd have to set a budget first. A firm budget."

Mia nodded in agreement, and Lindsey studied her, wondering what the heck was going on. This wasn't like Mia. She was usually more cautious and sensible. They were alike in that way.

"You know what would be really cool?" Shelby leaned forward. "Remember those three guys we met on our last day on Waikiki beach?"

"Uh, yeah," Mia said. "Smokin' hot."

Lindsey stiffened. "What about them?"

"What if we could get them to meet us?" Grinning, Shelby darted a mischievous look between them. "In Hawaii."

Rick. Oh, lord. Lindsey's stomach churned and for a moment she thought she really was going to be sick.

"How would we do that? We don't even know their last names." Mia snorted. "Not to mention they're probably married or in prison."

Shelby made a face at Mia, then ignored her completely. "We know what university they went to, so we use Facebook."

"Huh." Mia looked as if she were mulling it over. "We could send a message to the alumni group. It couldn't hurt."

"But they'll have to have signed up as alumni in order

to get the message." Lindsey clung to the hope that this crazy idea would fall apart. She couldn't see Rick again. Her friends didn't understand. She hadn't told them everything about that night.

Shelby shrugged. "Lots of people do. I have, haven't you?"

Mia shook her head. "Look, they answer, they don't, so what? It's Waikiki. We're bound to meet some gorgeous surfers who'll be ready to party."

"I like it." Shelby dug in her purse and produced a pen. "Anybody have a piece of paper or a dry napkin?"

Mia pulled her day planner out of her leather tote and tore off a used page. "Here."

"Oh, my God, they still have those things around? Why don't you use your BlackBerry?" Shelby found a clean spot on the table and started writing.

"I do both," Mia said, and glanced meaningfully at Lindsey, who Mia knew would normally appreciate the caution.

Right now, all Lindsey could think about was what it would be like to see Rick again, to feel his talented hands all over her body.

"Okay, how about something like this…" Shelby squinted as if she were having trouble reading her own writing. "Here we go… 'Remember spring break? Mia, Lindsey and Shelby will be at the Sea Breeze Hotel during the week of March whatever. Come if you dare. You know who you are.'"

"Not bad, but we'll have to be more specific." Mia did a quick mental calculation. "Remember spring break 2004."

"Right." Shelby scribbled in the correction. "Lindsey, what do you think?"

She shoved a hand through her hair and exhaled a shaky breath. It was dim in the bar. Maybe they couldn't see her blush all the way to her blond roots. "I think you'll have to change Lindsey to Jill."

Shelby blinked. "You didn't give him your real name?"

Lindsey slowly shook her head, and ignored the eruption of laughter. She was too busy panicking over seeing him again.

1

LINDSEY STEPPED OUT on the tiny balcony and let the clean fresh air bathe her skin. Like magic the tension melted from her body, and she strained over the railing, trying to get a glimpse of the ocean. They'd booked two adjoining mountain-view rooms, which meant they could see a small wedge of green mountain and lots of other hotels that crowded Waikiki. The price was right, though, and as nice as the ocean-view rooms would have been, Lindsey had insisted on sticking to their budget. How much time would they be spending there, anyway?

She gave up any hope of seeing the water, and gazed down at the profusion of pink, yellow and white plumerias that covered the trees around the hotel grounds. Inhaling deeply, she swore the flowers' perfume wafted all the way up to the seventh floor. Or maybe her senses had misfired, and what she remembered was the night on the beach when Rick had tucked one behind her right ear.

"Hey, Linds," Shelby called from the other room through the open connecting door. "Where did you go?"

Sighing, Lindsey left the balcony, closing the sliding glass door behind her. "What's up?"

Shelby, wrapped in a white hotel towel, ducked into the room, her long hair damp from her shower. "I thought maybe you went down to the bar with Mia."

"Nope. I was checking out the view."

"View?" Shelby's brows went up. "We have a view?" She grinned, her gaze taking in Mia's suitcase, which was sitting on the luggage rack, and then Lindsey's bag, which was stowed in the open closet. "How are we divvying up the bathrooms?"

"We're going to be adults and not hog either of them." Shoving aside a pile of Shelby's shorts, Lindsey found her brown leather purse. "I'm going to the gift shop to look for a pair of sunglasses."

"I saw one of those ABC stores on the corner. I bet they're cheaper there."

Lindsey eyed her friend. She wasn't the kind who normally thought about anything as pedestrian as price. "I'm so proud."

"Damn straight. I'll have you know I didn't go a penny over my clothes budget."

Lindsey sighed. It wouldn't have occurred to Shelby to make do with what she had, just as Lindsey and Mia had done. Okay, so Lindsey had splurged on a new sundress, but only because she could wear it to work once they opened Anything Goes. She wouldn't need her suits anymore. At least not for the next two years. That's how long she'd given herself to make a go of the business before she'd consider returning to her old company.

"You need anything from the store?" Lindsey asked, refusing to feel guilty for having a bailout plan. She'd be crazy not to protect her future in the event the business failed. Naturally she had faith they would kick butt, but just in case, it was good to have a backup. Which she did, thanks to her former boss, who said she would always be welcomed back.

"No, I'm good. I think I packed everything."

Lindsey snorted. "Uh, yeah, I think you did."

"Just wait until you need to borrow something because you forgot to pack it."

They'd been checked in for less than an hour and Shelby already had spread out, scattering heaps of clothes on the beds and dresser. It didn't matter. With any luck, none of them would be in the room much anyway.

Naturally that thought led to Rick. Was he here? Had he even seen the Facebook shout-out? Even if he had, why would he have given it a second thought? They'd known each other for eight measly hours. A guy like him probably met women on the beach all the time. Making love to them under the moon and stars was no big deal.

That night had meant everything to her. He'd been the second guy she'd been with, and he'd shown her what the fuss was all about. Jeez, she could still remember how she'd come apart at the seams. In all the years since, she hadn't felt anything like it. "I'm gonna go," she said. "Are you meeting Mia in the bar?"

"I've got to put away my stuff and dry my hair." Shelby shook out a blue halter top. "What about you?"

"I don't know yet. Eventually we'll meet up." She wanted to be alone when she saw Rick. *If* she saw him. *Please, God, let her see him.* She slipped her purse strap onto her shoulder and headed for the door. "See you later."

"Oh, Linds—"

"I won't forget the bronzing lotion." Without a backward glance, Lindsey smiled and checked the outside pocket of her purse for her key card before shutting the door behind her.

She had the elevator to herself and used the few seconds to study her pale legs, her unpolished toenails. Maybe she shouldn't have worn shorts yet. If she'd had the time she would've hit a tanning salon and gotten a pedicure, but between easing out of her job and packing up her apartment, she'd been busy up to the last minute.

The elevator doors slid open and she stepped into the lobby, greeted by the tangy salt air and a buzzing group of Asian tourists. She quickly got out of their way so they could board the elevator, and then paused until she got her bearings. The lobby opened out to the beach, and she gazed at the white sand and crystal blue water, the late afternoon sun sinking on the horizon, so beautiful, so soothing. This was her week to chill, to find bliss with or without Rick. She was meant to be here. This was perfect.

Even walking to the store would be a pleasure. Everything smelled of the sea and suntan lotion, every view was a treat, and there were men here, lots of them, so it was all good. With a final look, she turned around.

And saw Rick. Standing not ten feet away. Their gazes met and her heart swooped into a free fall. For all she'd hoped, she'd never believed, but it was him, all right.

He hadn't changed much. In fact, wearing tan cargo

shorts and a black T-shirt, he looked as if he still belonged on a college campus. His light brown hair was still long, maybe more sun-streaked, his shoulders broad, his skin a deeper bronze. His mouth curved into that slow, killer smile she'd dreamed about for six years.

"Jill," he said in a voice huskier than she recalled.

She blinked, swallowed. "Rick." Before she knew what was happening, she was wrapped in his arms and he'd lifted her off the floor.

She clung to his shoulders for support, muscles bunching under her palms. Oh, he'd definitely filled out. Her heart beat wildly as he spun her around, both of them grinning like kids. A moment passed, then two, and she was aware once more of the crowded lobby, of how tightly he held her against his body.

"Everybody's looking," she said with a shaky laugh.

"Let 'em." He set her down, and lowered his head for a kiss that merely brushed her cheek. "You look great."

She combed a self-conscious hand through her hair. "I didn't expect to see you."

A brief frown darkened his hazel eyes. "Facebook— that was you, right?"

"Yes." Her purse strap had slid down her shoulder, and she twisted it around her hand. "I meant that I just checked in, and well, here you are."

He winked with that same casual confidence she'd admired before. "I couldn't wait."

Unfortunately, her attempt to sound casual came out as a small strangled laugh. He seemed taller than six feet but that had to be wrong because he'd been twenty-three when they'd first met, past the growing stage. Of course, they hadn't been vertical much. The thought made her blush. Darn him for catching her off guard. She'd needed time to slip into Jill mode. Shoot, she needed to give him her real name. *That* was going to be fun.

"You feel like catching up?" he added.

"Sure."

He took her hand, which affected her far more than it should have. When she saw he was taking her to the Plantation Bar, she put on the brakes and shook her hand free.

Rick cocked a brow. "Something wrong?"

"How about the bar at the pool?"

"The Plantation Bar might be quieter."

"One of my friends is there," Lindsey admitted. "I'd rather be alone."

He took her hand back and changed direction. The thrill was just as strong. *Come on, Lindsey, get a grip, it's just holding hands, for goodness' sake.* If he—really—kissed her, she'd probably pass out. She wished she'd gotten the sunglasses though because she couldn't stop staring at him. He wasn't just hot. He'd left hot in the dust and gone straight to burning. In her dreams, he'd been yummy, but not nearly this tanned or ripped and, *he hadn't been able to wait!*

Sand between her toes surprised her into stopping. She looked down at her sandals and then at Rick. They were on the beach and not headed to the pool, which was in the other direction. "Rick—"

"I know this cool bar on the beach. You won't run in to anybody there." He flashed a dazzling smile. "Unless you left more than one broken heart here six years ago."

Even though she knew he was teasing, her breath caught anyway. "I lost count."

His grin broadened. "It's so good to see you, Jill."

"I have something to tell you."

"What's that?"

"My name isn't Jill." She cleared her throat. "It's Lindsey."

An odd expression crossed his face, and she had the horrible feeling that he was about to walk away, leave her standing in the middle of the beach. He only kicked off his brown flip-flops, and then stooped to pick them up. "That's going to take some getting used to. You want to take off those sandals?"

"That's it?"

"You can take your top off if you want."

"No." Heat crawled up her neck. "No, I meant about me giving you a fake name."

His smile told her that he'd been teasing again. She seriously needed to loosen up.

"You were being cautious." He shrugged. "I get it... Lindsey." He said her name slowly, as if trying it out. "I like Lindsey. It suits you."

"Good." She felt better...except for her feet. The sand lodged between her arches and sandals felt gritty and uncomfortable. She slipped the sandals off before they continued down the beach.

"Are you going to tell me your last name?" He playfully bumped her shoulder with his. "Or do you want to wait and see how the day goes?"

"Not a bad idea."

A faint smile lifted the corners of his mouth. "Mine is Granger."

She had to give him points for not reacting badly to the fake name. "Shaw." But she wouldn't give him her room number yet. "When did you get here?"

"The end of November."

"I meant Hawaii."

"I know." He jerked his chin toward a hotel bordering the beach and guided her in that direction. "I have a house here."

"In Waikiki?"

"The other side of the island. On the North Shore."

She shook her head, totally confused. She knew he'd gone to school in Southern California, and that he was from Michigan. "When did you move here?"

"I didn't." He shaded his eyes and gazed out over the ocean, briefly focusing on a couple of bodysurfers. "I'm only here part-time. This is it," he said, gesturing.

The bar was little more than a grass hut without walls. She'd seen it from a distance and thought it was a concession that rented out surfboards and canoes. But there were shelves of liquor in the center, surrounded by a wooden bar and wooden stools. Inside the circle, a big man wearing a yellow Hawaiian shirt garnished frothy drinks with pineapple wedges and cherries.

The bartender looked up when they slid onto stools facing the water, and a grin softened his craggy features. "Hey, Rick, long time no see. What you doin' on this side of da island, bruddah?"

"Slumming."

The man chuckled, leaned closer as he picked up the glasses. "You right about that," he said in a discreet voice, giving Lindsey a quick wink before carrying the order to the customers sitting at the other end of the bar.

"Slumming?" Lindsey repeated.

Rick swiveled around to face her, his legs spread, effectively trapping her. "Not you. It's a tourist thing."

"I'm a tourist."

He picked up a lock of her hair and rubbed it between his fingers in a surprisingly intimate gesture. "I can't believe you're here," he murmured.

"I figured you'd have forgotten about me by the next day."

He let go of her hair, met her gaze. "Why did you disappear without waking me up?"

Lindsey tensed, unprepared to explain herself, unwilling to admit that he'd frightened her by making her feel things she'd never dreamed possible. "I woke up late. I didn't want to miss my plane, and I honestly didn't think it mattered. You knew I was leaving."

He studied her a minute, then shrugged. "I figured it was something like that." He swiveled back around just as the bartender approached. "When did you start working here? I thought you were at the Hyatt."

"I'm workin' two jobs. Gotta pay da bills, bruddah."

"Yeah, I hear you," Rick said, and the older man's brown eyes glinted with amusement she didn't quite understand. "This is Lindsey, Keoni."

Keoni acknowledged her with a nod. "What can I get you?" he asked, and then said to Rick, "Beer for you, I know."

Lindsey thought for a moment. "That sounds good."

Rick's brows went up. "No fancy drink?"

"They have a way of sneaking up on me," she admitted.

Keoni had already moved away to grab mugs, but she saw him smile.

Rick turned back to face her, this time taking one of her hands and lightly pressing it between his slightly callused ones.

"I don't want you drunk," he murmured in a low voice meant only for her ears.

She started to laugh, thinking he was teasing, but his hazel eyes were serious. "I wasn't drunk last time, if that's what you're implying."

"No—" He looked as if he wanted to say something else, but Keoni slid their mugs in front of them. "Thanks."

He might have stuck around, but a young couple came up from the beach and pulled out stools, and Lindsey watched Keoni amble toward them.

Rick stroked her palm with his thumb. The pad wasn't smooth like that of a desk jockey. When they'd met he'd been an engineering student. She wondered if he'd finished school, or decided he'd rather hang out at the beach.

"I wish I'd known Keoni was working here," he muttered. "Nice guy, but I was hoping for a bartender I wouldn't know, so we'd be alone like you said."

She slowly swung her gaze to his face.

His lips twitched. "To talk."

"Of course." She looked deeply into his eyes, entranced by the way the hazel had become a warm gold. Her breathing slipped slightly off-kilter, and as hard as she struggled to look away, she couldn't.

"Screw it." He leaned in and kissed her.

Not a quick one, either. He lingered, slanting his

mouth over hers, his lips supple and coaxing. Startled, her senses swimming, she felt the tip of his tongue tease the corner of her mouth, and she parted her lips.

He slid his tongue inside, slow and hot and demanding, making her forget where they were. He moved his hand to her thigh, up high, where her shorts ended. His thumb slid just under the hem. Coming from somewhere in the haze she heard a woman's faint laugh.

Lindsey froze, and realized with an element of shock that they were sitting at the bar in full view.

She broke away, not knowing where to look, what to do. She wanted to hide her face in her hands. Instead, she grabbed blindly for her mug and took a long cool sip of beer.

"Relax," Rick said, his hand still resting on her thigh. "Lots of honeymooners around. No one even noticed."

She kept her hands wrapped around the mug, and stared down at the amber brew. It wasn't the kiss, exactly, that had her flustered. It was how quickly the fire inside her had ignited, how quickly the heat had surged through her veins and settled low in her belly. It seemed almost unnatural.

Good grief, it wasn't as if she'd been living in a convent for the past six years. There had been other men she'd liked, a couple of them well enough to have become intimate with, but no one had ever made her feel as if nothing around her mattered, as if the only reason for her next breath was to feel his touch again. But wasn't that exactly why she was here? She wanted to relive those eight hours, stretch them out to a week.

Rick reached for his beer. After taking a sip, he rested

an elbow on the bar and just looked at her. "So where are you living these days?"

A giggle rose in her throat. After that kiss, the question struck her as ridiculously funny. "Chicago." She cleared her throat. "No, New York, I guess."

"You guess?"

"I'm in the process of moving."

His brows drew together in a frown that said he didn't believe her.

She'd already lied to him about her name. It wasn't a stretch to think she didn't want him to know where she lived. "It's the truth."

A smile tugged at one side of his mouth, and his gaze fell to her lips.

Her heart thumped wildly.

Excellent. He was going to kiss her again.

2

LINDSEY, RICK REMINDED himself as he watched her nervously moisten her lips, not Jill. It was going to take some serious mental gear-shifting for her real name to sink in. If he hadn't thought about her over the years, it might've been different. But that night on the beach had turned into more than a simple one-time hookup. Should've been nothing more, he knew. He'd had his share of them. Went with the lifestyle. In his sphere, chicks loved surfers. And if a guy was lucky enough to make money at it, the women seemed all the more willing.

"Were you transferred?" he asked, steeling himself against the fathomless depths of her blue eyes. Damn, he wanted to kiss her again.

She blinked. "What?"

"Your job was in Chicago. Now you're moving to New York."

"Oh, yes, I mean no." She wrinkled her nose, something she seemed to do when she was frustrated with herself. He liked it. "I wasn't transferred. I quit."

"Yeah? What kind of job was it?"

"Accounting."

He hadn't seen that coming. Sticking her behind a desk seemed like a huge waste. With her long blond hair and big innocent blue eyes, she was a stunner. Great body, too. Not as skinny as six years ago. Her hips and breasts seemed more filled out. But he couldn't let his mind go there, not yet. "Tired of corporate America, huh? Man, I get that."

"I liked the company I worked for. They're old and stable and have a great pension plan.…" Her voice trailed off, and she briefly looked down at her hands. "I'm going into business with my college friends, Mia and Shelby. You didn't meet them last time."

"Good for you. Taking a small risk now and then is good for the soul."

"Small risk?" She let out a laugh.

He grinned. "Ah, right, the pension plan."

"Having no income until we make a profit?" she said defensively. "Excuse me, but that's more than a small risk."

"You're right." He held up his hands. "My bad."

"What about you? What have you been doing?"

"A lot of surfing lately, though we've probably seen the last of the really big waves for the season."

"I meant work."

"I know." He paused, watched Keoni schmooze with his customers. "The prize money for competition surfing is pretty good. It usually carries me through the year." He shrugged. "Since I'm flexible, I spend a few months on the mainland, see my family, go skiing."

The questions in her eyes multiplied. No surprise there. He was twenty-nine. Most people figured at that age a man should settle down, start thinking about a career, family. They weren't necessarily wrong, but he had too much to do yet.

"Weren't you an engineering student?" she asked, more curious than judgmental, which he appreciated.

"Yep, got my degree, checked out the job market, managed to get a few offers." He took a swallow of beer. "But I just couldn't see myself sitting in an office watching the clock." He leaned back. "You look surprised."

"I am. You seemed excited about going into engineering."

Rick chuckled. "I *was* excited." He stroked the silky smooth skin just below the hem of her shorts. "It had nothing to do with engineering."

She blushed. Something else he liked about her. Women didn't seem to do that anymore. "You're bad," she muttered, and brought the mug to her lips. She took a small sip and smiled.

Keoni returned, grabbing the towel that was draped over his beefy shoulder and mopped the moisture their mugs left on the bar. With a jerk of his broad chin, he asked Rick, "You ready for another one?"

"Nah, I have to drive."

Keoni shrugged, saw that a customer at the far end of the bar was signaling for his check and started backing away. "How's the shoulder?"

"A little stiff." Rick gingerly touched the spot where he'd gotten banged up. "Not too bad."

"Don't be stupid about it, brah. You'll end up bartending, like me."

Rick watched him paste on a smile for the customer and pass the man his tab. No, Rick wouldn't end up being a bartender, forcing smiles for the tourists, even if he quit surfing tomorrow. He might be easygoing but he wasn't foolish. He'd made sure he was set for life. Not that it was anyone's business. The more people knew about him, the more they expected of him. He didn't need that crap.

"What's wrong with your shoulder?" Lindsey asked, her eyes filled with concern.

"I hurt it a while ago. It's good now."

Her gaze touched his shoulder, moved to his chest, slid down to his belly. Then her high small breasts rose and fell with her soft sigh.

They needed to find some privacy. "Let's go," he said, and she eagerly nodded.

He pulled a twenty out of his pocket, slapped it down on the bar, anchored it with his mug and grabbed her hand.

LINDSEY WAS PRETTY SURE the few sips of beer wasn't what was making her light-headed. It was Rick. The feel of his palm pressing hers, the way his long lean fingers curled possessively around her hand, the warm masculine scent of his body, all of it made her squishy inside. She liked that he'd shaved recently, and that his jaw was nice and smooth, and the cleft in his chin so prominent without whiskers to detract from it.

Even the glossiness of his sun-kissed hair in the sunlight and the bronze glow of his skin got to her in a surprisingly primal way. He had perfect posture, too, which was almost as important to her as good hygiene. She had fairly stringent requirements when it came to men, she suddenly realized. Or had she been comparing her subsequent dates to him?

No, that wasn't possible. She'd known him for one night. An incredible, earth-stopping night, but still.

"How about we go to my place?" he asked when they were halfway back to the hotel.

She should have anticipated this, but she hadn't thought ahead. "How far away is it?"

"About an hour, a little more depending on traffic."

Her gaze went to the horizon. It was still light out, but the weakening sun was already sinking toward the water. "It would be dark by the time we got back."

He tugged her closer. "You could spend the night."

"I can't," she said quickly. "We just arrived today. My friends and I—I don't want to ditch them our first night here."

"Sure, no problem." After a pause, he said, "How about I take you all to dinner?"

"I don't know." Lindsey knew she wasn't ready for everyone to meet just yet. Not until she and Rick became reacquainted themselves. Hesitantly, she said, "I can check with them."

"They might be busy. If I saw the Facebook thing, I'm sure a lot of other guys did, too."

She nodded, and dug in her bag for her phone. "I'll text them and see what's going on."

He released her hand, the abruptness startling her. Then he reached out and snatched a red Frisbee that was sailing through the air, headed straight for her.

The two boys, who'd been tossing the disc back and forth, stared warily at them.

Rick held on to the Frisbee while they approached the kids. "It's too breezy and unpredictable to be playing with this on a crowded beach, guys," he told them gently. "Why don't you take it over there?" He indicated a strip of barren sand that stretched out between two hotels. "I'll throw it to you."

He waited until they'd run toward the spot, and with a small flick of his wrist, sent the Frisbee sailing over the boys' outstretched arms.

"Whoa," both kids yelled in unison, and turned to scramble after the toy.

"I see you've had some practice," she commented, quickly finishing her brief message, then pressing Send.

"I play with my nieces and nephews when I'm home. They gang up on me."

"Poor baby. How many do you have?"

"Seems like a hundred." He shrugged, his fondness for them evident in his reluctant smile. "Five, all together. Three of them are a year apart and never run out of energy."

She laughed, glanced at her phone, hoping Mia or Shelby would get back to her right away, or better yet, were too busy to respond.

"Tell you what," he said, "if your friends are busy, why don't we grab a picnic dinner and eat on the beach while we watch the sun set. There's a cool place about ten minutes from here. No tourists."

"Thanks," she said dryly.

Grinning, he slid an arm around her waist. "Some tourists I like." He nuzzled the side of her neck. "One in particular, I like very much."

His warm moist breath caressed her skin, giving

her goose bumps. "Okay…I think I gave the girls long enough."

He drew back, regarding her with an amused quirk of his brow. "You sure?"

"Yes, I am," she said, and hoped she was right.

THE TRIP TO THE small market near the Honolulu zoo was an adventure all by itself. Most of the customers were friendly locals who apparently lived nearby and were doing their weekly shopping. The shelves were stocked with the normal basic staples, but there was also a large assortment of Asian foods that Lindsey simply couldn't identify. Half the labels were of no help since she couldn't read Chinese or Japanese.

Fortunately Rick seemed to know what he was doing. Or so she hoped, as she watched him toss a variety of items into the basket. At the ready-made section, he asked her to choose what she'd like. She pointed at something she assumed was made with rice, marinated chicken and cucumbers, and crossed her fingers.

While they stood in line at the checkout, she found a rack of sunglasses and tried on a couple. The selection was limited and mostly they were too big, but she settled on a cute enough, reasonably priced pair just as it was their turn to pay. She sidled up next to Rick, and dug in her purse for her wallet.

"I'm paying," she said.

He frowned at her. "No, you aren't."

"It's fair. You bought our drinks at the bar."

"Not gonna happen." He pulled out a wad of bills from his pocket.

The cashier scanned the last item, and Lindsey

stubbornly was about to give the woman her debit card when Rick tossed a large box of condoms onto the counter.

"Could you get that, too," he told the woman.

Lindsey froze, her gaze glued to the box. The really, really big box.

The cashier obliged him, then gave Rick a total, for which he handed her cash.

She felt like an idiot. No reason a grown woman should be embarrassed about buying condoms, but at a grocery store? Come on. The stooped Asian lady waiting in line behind them had to be older than Lindsey's grandmother.

"Hey." Rick picked up their two bags. "Did you want to get those sunglasses? I'm sorry I didn't see them in your hands."

"They aren't right for me," she said, hastily putting them back in their slot, and then leading him out of the store.

When they got to his Jeep, he carefully stowed the groceries on the floor in the back, while she slid into the passenger's seat and buckled herself in. He climbed in behind the wheel, inserted the key into the ignition but didn't start the engine.

"I embarrassed you back there. I'm sorry. I wasn't thinking."

"What are you talking about?" she asked, all innocence, and felt the heat rise from her neck to her face.

Rick chuckled, snatched her hand and pressed a quick kiss on the back of it before starting the engine. "We have to hurry or we'll miss the best part of the sunset."

After about ten minutes, they drove through a residential area where the houses were huge and spread out on mammoth lots, and reminded Lindsey of the mansions that once lorded over old sugar plantations.

They hadn't gone far when Rick pulled off and drove them down a short gravel road and parked. On the right there was a small shabby house, to the left nothing but scrub brush and tall graceful palms swaying in the stiff ocean breeze. Before them lay a field of grass that butted up to a sandy beach.

He hopped out of the Jeep and pocketed the keys. "I'll get the food. You take the mat and towels."

"Isn't this private property?"

"Nope. Public access to the beach."

She came around the back of the car. There was no trunk, and she spotted the rolled-up straw mat and a couple of towels stashed on the backseat. She saw he kept a small cooler there, too, and watched as he dumped in a bag of ice he'd bought. With swift efficiency, he packed in cans of cola and beer, and then laid the cheese and fruit on top. He left the warm ready-made items and box of crackers in the paper sacks, and then handed her the mat and towels.

"I can handle the bag, too," she said, and grabbed the handles when she saw that he'd planned on balancing it on top of the cooler chest.

"Thanks, we're not going far." His hands full, he used his knee to shut the door, and her gaze automatically drifted to the ridge of muscle that went up his thigh and disappeared under his shorts. "Ready?"

She cleared her throat and promptly lifted her gaze. "Yep."

They got to the grass where there was an actual path to follow to a long stretch of solitary beach. In the distance, one hotel after another loomed against the dusky sky. To the right, toward the center of the island, white and gray clouds shrouded the tops of huge green mountains.

"Do those look like rain clouds to you?" she asked.

"I don't think so. If it does come down, the rain will stay close to the mountains. We're going this way," he said, gesturing to their left. "Toward Diamond Head."

Up this close, the crater wasn't as visible as it was from the hotel, but she'd been curious about it since her first trip. "How did it get its name?"

"Diamond Head? I think it dates back to the eighteen hundreds. British sailors mistook the crystals embedded in the rocks for diamonds. The ancient Hawaiians called it Leahi, but nowadays everybody refers to it as Diamond Head."

"What does Leahi mean?"

"The 'ahi' part means tuna. Some local people will swear it means brow of the tuna, others say it's the fin of the tuna." He shrugged. "You can't tell from here, but it looks like a fin to me."

She watched him take a lingering look, as if he never got tired of the scene. "You really love it here."

"I like the people, and to me there's no better surfing than on the North Shore. But I still get rock fever between trips to the mainland."

"I've heard the term before, not sure what it means."

"Nothing changes. The weather is pretty much the same year round, except for the rainier months. I'm used to the leaves changing color in October, the first snowfall, skiing, all that seasonal stuff."

"Yeah, by January I'm complaining about the cold but I'd miss the change of seasons, too." She squinted at the expanse of beach ahead of them, wishing she'd bought the darn sunglasses. "How far are we going?"

"Almost there."

She honestly didn't see the difference between one spot to the next. Once they'd made it past the grassy field there was nothing but sand and scrub. But she said nothing when he kept walking. After a few more yards and he stopped, gazed out at the water and then kicked away some branches before setting down the cooler.

"This particular spot reserved for you?" she asked with a grin.

"You'll thank me in a few minutes." He took the bag from her and set it on top of the cooler before shaking out the straw mat, something that seemed to be a tourist staple.

Lindsey frowned, curious as to what he meant. While he laid out one of the beach towels, she scanned the horizon. A large ship that she'd assumed was on the move had actually anchored. Their opportunity to see the sun sinking out of view could have been ruined depending on where they'd chosen to plant themselves.

Rick lifted the cooler onto the corner of the mat, and then spread out one of the beach towels. She should have offered to help instead of staring, but she couldn't seem to help herself. The fluid ripple of muscle in his legs and arms as he moved held her captive. She hadn't thought it possible, but Rick was better looking than she'd remembered.

She moistened her suddenly parched lips, her gaze sweeping the beach. Anticipation with a dash of apprehension swirled like freshly churned butter inside her.

It seemed she had him all to herself.

3

RICK FINISHED SETTING UP, then looked up at Lindsey. She hadn't moved, just stood there quietly staring at him. He had no idea what was going through her head. Except that she seemed to have drifted off into another world, maybe another time. Like to that night six years ago when they had lain naked in the moonlight, kissing, making love, whispering secrets.

He had trouble not going there himself. Hard to do since it was way up there on the memorable-nights scale. Her blond hair was slightly shorter now, but still long enough that he itched to see it tousled and tumbling over her shoulders as she straddled him, rode him until he couldn't hold back another second.

Not until she blinked and looked away did it occur to him that he was staring, too.

"Is this beach always so quiet?" she asked, gazing toward the ocean.

"I wish." He got to his feet. "At one time only the locals knew about it. But most of the houses around here are rentals now so that increased the tourist traffic."

"It's still a lot nicer than the hotel beaches." Her eyes widened suddenly, and she rubbed her arms.

He knew exactly what she was thinking. "This isn't the beach where we…you know," he said. "I thought about going there, but lately this one is more private."

She gave a small nod. "It's gotten a bit cool."

"This from a woman who just left Chicago in March?"

"I was dressed more appropriately." She held out her arms, indicating her red tank top as confirmation. Good thing she hadn't looked down. Even though she wasn't braless, her distended nipples poked at the thin fabric.

He had to turn his head. From the first moment he'd seen her, it hadn't taken much to set him off. "Come here." He lowered himself onto the mat and spread his legs, leaving enough room for her to sit in front of him. He patted the spot. "You can lean back against me."

She hesitated, and then with a slightly shy smile, she sat down and drew her bent knees to her chest.

"Scoot back more," he said when she'd left too much space between them.

"I don't want to crowd you."

Smiling at her naiveté, he wrapped his arms around her, bent knees and all, and pulled her against his chest. She hadn't changed much from the shy sexy college student he'd met that night. He'd hadn't dared hope she could still be the same sweet girl that had summoned every ounce of courage to get naked on the beach, and have sex with a guy she'd just met. But then they had connected in a big way in those predawn hours. He'd told her things.…

He deeply inhaled her vanilla scent. "Warmer?" he asked, tightening his arms around her.

Her contented sigh went straight to his cock. "Perfect," she said, relaxing against him.

He kissed her soft blond hair, then moved so that his cheek pressed hers. "Doesn't seem like it's been six years."

"I was just thinking the same thing."

"I figured you'd be married by now."

"Seriously?" She shifted, and glanced over her shoulder at him. "Why would you think that?"

He shrugged, kept his gaze on the horizon, not keen on getting too deep into that conversation. "I was shocked to see your message on Facebook. A lot of people I went to school with are making that trip to the altar lately."

"Same here. I received two wedding invitations from sorority sisters last week." She settled back against him.

"No one can find me so they send invitations to my parents' house in Michigan. My mom forwards my mail every two weeks."

"That's because you're such a nomad."

"Not true. I still spend a lot of time at the old homestead. I'd be there now if I hadn't seen your message."

"Really?" She straightened again, twisting around to look at him with those big blue eyes. "You stayed for me?"

"I did."

"I'm so glad."

"Me, too. Look." He pointed toward the sun, partially hidden behind a pink cloud, the sky a golden glow. As far as sunsets went, this one wasn't spectacular. There weren't enough clouds to give them a real show. But he couldn't keep looking into those soft blue eyes without saying something stupid.

Holding her, smelling her vanilla-scented hair and thinking back to that night when he'd been emotionally stripped was freaking him out a little.

Lindsey had turned just twenty-one, and unlike most of her college friends, she'd been endearingly old-fashioned. Enough that he'd asked outright if she was a virgin. She'd gotten all flustered as she'd insisted she wasn't. He grinned as he remembered her blush. She'd been ready to run from him. With soft kisses and gentle words he'd convinced her to stay.

He'd always been good at that kind of persuasion, good with women, period. Even in high school, he'd had the touch. He'd been with college girls, which hadn't made him too popular with the guys in school. Luckily, he'd always been a loner, shying away from the beaten path or the mundane. His sister had always said his propensity to become bored would be his downfall.

He wasn't bored with Lindsey. She'd blown him away that night with her quiet conviction, her unshakable vision of her future. The long blond hair and small perfect breasts hadn't hurt, but there was more to it than that. She'd surprised him, first with her innocence, then with her strength. Even tonight, though they'd barely been together a few hours, she had his complete attention.

She shifted again, and he loosened his hold so that she could stretch her legs out in front of her. He smiled when she took his arms and pulled them back in place. This time, with her knees out of the way, his arms fit nicely crossed just below her breasts.

He tried using his chin to push the hair away from her neck, and when that didn't work, she got the hint and draped the thick locks over the front of her shoulder. With better access to her neck, he kissed the side, then bit at her earlobe. She giggled and squirmed.

"I thought you liked that," he whispered.

"I do, but it still tickles."

"And this?" He lightly dragged the tip of his tongue around the shell of her ear.

She squirmed more, the proximity of her cute little ass to his cock sheer torture. He moved one of his arms until it grazed the underside of her breasts. He knew the second she'd sucked in a breath. Slowly she let it out.

"It's so beautiful here," she said, "and peaceful."

"Let's hope it stays that way."

She turned her head to look toward Waikiki, and he studied her profile, admiring the way her full lower lip jutted slightly. Her lashes were thick, and he could tell that she'd tried to artificially darken her eyebrows with makeup. But overall she was light on the cosmetics, which suited him. He liked the more natural look.

"I don't see anyone headed this way," she said.

"We're safe. No waves so the local surfing crowd won't be showing up, and it's dinnertime for everyone else."

"What do you mean no waves?"

"That?" He followed her gaze to the small swells that quickly lost momentum before the break. "Those aren't waves. Not even a self-respecting bodysurfer would waste his time on those ripples."

Lindsey grinned. "Well, aren't we cocky?"

"Wait until we get to the other side of the island,

you'll see what I mean. Too bad you weren't here in December and January when the big waves hit."

"Were you already surfing when we first met?"

"For a couple of years, mostly on weekends. I lived near Hermosa Beach in Southern California while going to school."

"You never mentioned it—surfing, I mean."

"I believe we had better things to do." Rick nuzzled her neck, and murmured against her skin, "Like now."

She made a small mewing sound and leaned back, running her palm over his forearms. She had small hands, tiny wrists. Her skin was pale against his. He had to make sure she took care not to burn in the midday sun.

He moved his hand and cupped her left breast through her tank top. She didn't stiffen as he'd suspected she might, but only sighed. Damn, he wished they were back at his place. Within twenty minutes it would be dark except for the half moon. He had no problem stripping down right here, but he knew she would. And he wanted to see her in the worst way.

He abandoned her breast, moved his hand down. When he slipped it underneath her top, she tensed. But she let him stroke the soft skin over her rib cage, and she even turned her head so that her eyelashes fluttered against his temple. He found her bra, and released the front clasp, then covered her mouth with his.

HER NIPPLES WERE ALREADY beaded and hard, but the shock of the first touch jolted her, making her tear away from his kiss and scan the beach. Murmuring a reassurance, he used his free hand to bring her mouth back to his. She didn't resist. She felt too weak and hot and hope-lessly needy. The touch of his roughened fingers against her sensitive nipple made her quiver, and a whimper escaped from her lips into his mouth.

She was a mess, an utter and complete mess, and he'd barely touched her. She had to slow him down. Slow down her own growing desire to touch him, to feel the hard contour of his muscled arms and chest against her skin. It was too light out. Anyone could walk up and surprise them. That would ruin everything.

Lindsey broke from him again, evading his hand when he tried to pull her back. "Rick."

He palmed her breast, whispered something she didn't understand, his warm breath skimming her ear.

Her eyes drifted closed, only for an instant, and he lightly pinched her nipple. "Rick. No."

Before the word was fully formed, he'd stopped. His hand slid out from under her top. "Lindsey, I'm sorry," he said, the remorse in his voice thick.

"Oh, wait." Leaving the comfort of his arms, she twisted around to see him. He looked devastated. "That wasn't a don't-ever-do-that-again no," she said, briefly touching his face. "It was more a I'm-a-big-fat-chicken no because it's too light out."

A relieved smile totally transformed his expression.

She laughed softly. "I like you touching me," she whispered, and watched his expression change again.

His nostrils flared, his jaw tightened. "Good." His heated gaze went briefly to her breasts before lifting to meet her eyes. "I plan on doing a lot of that."

She tried to control the shiver that rattled her insides, shook the starch out of her spine. But it was too late. She only hoped her voice wouldn't fail her. "We should eat. Before it's too dark."

He ran his hand up her arm. "Your bra," he said, keeping his eyes level with hers.

"My bra?" She frowned, glanced down at her chest. Her unbound breasts. Her aroused nipples. "Oh." She reached under her tank top and fumbled with the clasp.

"You're killing me," he said with a shaky laugh, and pushed off the mat, getting to his feet in a flash. "Cola or beer?" he asked, without looking at her.

"Cola." She finished fastening the clasp, in spite of her unsteady fingers, and wondered if it would be fair to ask him to take off his shirt.

She supposed she had a normal sexual appetite typical for a woman her age, but she never obsessed over a man's body like she'd been doing with Rick. But then she didn't personally know any guys who looked like *that*.

He handed her the opened can, then popped the cap off his bottle of beer. He threw his head back to take a long pull, and she seized the unguarded moment to stare at his fly. Her mouth went dry. He was still hard, impressively hard.

She averted her gaze and guzzled the cola. Maybe she should try calling Mia and Shelby, see if they were going to be out this evening and if one of the rooms would be free.

"I'd give just about anything to know what you're thinking."

Lindsey looked up into his amused face, and instinctively her hand went to her warm cheek. Silently, she cursed herself, as if she could do a darn thing about the persistent blushing. It so wasn't fair.

She blithely pressed the cold can against her heated skin. "Not in this lifetime."

Rick grinned. "After it gets dark we can go swimming, help cool you off."

"We don't have swimsuits," she said, choosing to ignore his teasing. "At least I don't."

"Hence, the after-dark part."

She laughed. "You did not just say that."

"What?"

"Hence?" She tried to stand, but had a bit of trouble with the loose sand, and accepted the hand he offered.

She gained her footing, and he could've released her. He didn't. He pulled her close, and she felt the heat of his arousal right through her clothes. She tilted her head back and waited for him to lower his mouth. He lightly brushed his lips over hers, then gradually increased the pressure, leisurely kissing her.

Her eyelids fluttered closed, blotting out the pinkish-gold twilight sky, blotting out everything but the feel of his muscled shoulder beneath her fingers. Her ability to reason evaporated on the sea breeze. If he wanted to make love to her right now, right here, she wouldn't resist.

Slowly he lifted his mouth. She opened her eyes to find him staring down at her. She almost begged him not to stop.

"Let's eat, huh?" he said, and with a gentle hand, freed the tendrils of hair that had tangled with her lashes.

She almost laughed. How could he be thinking about

food? She nodded, swiftly backed up and looked away, hoping he hadn't seen the disappointment in her eyes.

He used the other towel, and spread out the goodies he'd bought, being careful to anchor down anything that could blow away. After emptying the paper sack, he said, "We'll use this for all the recyclables. I'll sort them later." He indicated the empty plastic bag that had held the ice. "Trash can go in here."

Lindsey smiled.

"Go ahead," he said, with a bring-it-on cock of his brow. "I've already heard every smart-ass remark there is about how anal I am when it comes to recycling."

"Actually, I was thinking that there's enough food here for five people."

He patted his flat belly. "I've been known to eat for four."

"Hard to believe."

"I work it off."

"Surfing?"

"That, too," he said, and winked.

Lindsey gave him her best eye-roll, and hoped that he didn't see the pulse zinging at her wrist and neck. She was going to have to have sex with him soon, no matter where they ended up. Just so she could relax. Knowing it was coming, remembering how he had made her feel that one incredible night, was keeping her teetering on the edge.

"How should we do this?" she asked, staring down at the food, and not seeing any plates or utensils.

"No rules here." He sat down cross-legged, facing the food-laden towel as if it were a set table, and patted the spot beside him.

She joined him, and then helped by opening the box of crackers and container of cut-up fruit. He used a pocket knife to cut slices of cheese, stopping to hold a bit of the soft gouda to her lips.

She opened, and used her tongue to sweep the small piece into her mouth. "Mmm. Good."

He briefly kissed her, and then licked his lips. "My favorite."

She shook her head, pretending she wasn't amazed at the laid-back way he treated everything. Not her. The lightest kiss, the casual teasing, all made her stomach jittery. She focused on their dinner, eyed the ready-made food that she couldn't identify. "Any minute it's going to be too dark to see what we're eating."

Rick smiled. "Are you adventurous?"

"Define what—" She sighed, and went with the simple truth. "No."

He removed a pair of chopsticks from a paper wrapper. "Then it's better you don't see what's coming."

She grabbed one of the plastic forks that had been bundled with the chopsticks. "Uh, I'm not putting anything strange in my mouth."

His lips twitched. "What a pity."

She started to say something, thought better of it. She wasn't nearly quick enough to be witty, had never come up with—much less uttered—a double entendre in her life. There simply was no winning this conversation. She only wished blushing burned calories, but then she'd be a stick. She grabbed a couple of napkins and used them as a plate to hold the crackers while she topped them with cheese.

"You chose this one," he said, passing her the chicken and rice. "Adventurous or not, I think you'll like it."

Since she had made the selection, she opened it up and sampled the cucumber salad first. It was surprisingly good mixed with a sweet vinegary dressing. "I like this a lot," she said, spearing another cucumber half. "What's the black flecks on the rice?" She peered closer. They were too big to be black pepper.

"It's called furikake, a sesame seed-and-seaweed condiment. Don't make that face."

"Seaweed? Seriously?"

He nodded. "Try it."

She was a wuss when it came to trying ethnic food, but she figured a tiny taste wouldn't kill her. She forked a small portion, found the rice to be stickier than what she was accustomed to, but took a bite.

"Well?"

"Good." She watched him deftly use the chopsticks to scoop some kind of noodle salad into his mouth.

"Now try some chicken."

"What are you, my mother?"

Eyeing her, he chewed, swallowed, then set his chopsticks aside. Before she knew it, he cupped a hand behind her neck, drew her to him and gave her an openmouthed kiss. Not a long one, but intense enough to make her drop her fork.

"You tell me," he said with a cocky grin, and then went back to eating his dinner as if he'd merely suggested she check out the moon rising over the mountains.

4

THEY FINISHED DINNER, then stored what little food that was left over in the cooler along with the beer and colas. While Rick took the trash and recyclables to the car, Lindsey shook out the mat and towels. It was past nine, eerily dark and gloriously peaceful. The tropical air seemed cool for someone who'd recently flown in from frigid Chicago, but Lindsey was content to wrap herself in one of the thick blue towels as she settled on the mat and gazed up at the stars.

Rick hadn't suggested that they pack up and leave, and neither had she. They might've been more comfortable back at the hotel or sitting in the Jeep taking advantage of one of the many lookouts on this cliffy side of the island. She didn't think that either of them was trying to recapture that night they met. They simply didn't want the mood to shift, the talking and laughing to stop, the joy of sheer solitude to end.

Being with Rick again had affected her on so many levels. Like meeting up with an old friend you hadn't seen in years, yet immediately picking up where you'd left off. She wasn't surprised that she'd remembered him so vividly. Not with all the daydreams she'd had about him, especially the ones that came at night. What shocked her was his ease. As if he'd thought about her just as often. Somehow, knowing they were going to have sex rested between them easily. It shouldn't have. She was too shy, too awkward, but not with Rick.

He was so quiet she hadn't heard him approach. She caught a glimpse of his shadow in the sand a second before he dropped down beside her. Startled, her hand went to her throat.

"What's wrong?" He touched her hair, her shoulder, then rubbed the back of her neck. He liked touching.

She wasn't used to it. "I didn't hear you coming."

"You thought some other guy was on his way to kiss you until you begged for mercy?"

Lindsey smiled. "It happens."

He chuckled. "I remember the begging part, but it wasn't for mercy."

She bumped him with her shoulder. "You're awful."

He slid an arm around her and brought her to lean against him. "It's a cool breeze but the water is warm."

"Be my guest."

"I'm not going to talk you into going in, huh?"

"Nope." She shook her head for emphasis. They'd had this discussion at dinner. Oddly, she wasn't half as concerned about someone catching them in the buff as she was about swimming in the dark.

"We haven't seen anyone since we got here."

"It's not just that." She paused. The ocean was still a mystery to her. And in the dark? Forget it. He wouldn't understand. "Go on," she said. "I'll be waiting to wrap you in a nice warm towel." The thought of him stripping made her hot. Made her mouth dry. Oh, yeah, she liked where this was going. "Really, take a quick dip. I don't mind."

"Not without you."

"Then who would be waiting with the towel?"

His teeth gleamed in the moonlight. "You're trying to get me naked."

"Yes, I am," she said boldly, then ruined it by giggling.

"Hell, sweetheart, you only had to say the word."

Lindsey pressed her lips together to keep from blurting out something stupid. In the quiet, she heard a dog bark. "Oh, shoot."

"What?"

"I think someone's coming."

"Uh, a dog?"

"Someone might be walking the dog," she said in a hushed defensive voice, while straining to see in the murky light. The beach seemed clear on both sides, and she relaxed again.

"Satisfied?"

"I'm not the one getting naked."

"Oh, c'mon."

She smiled at the laughter in his voice, and briefly closed her eyes at the warm kiss he pressed to the side of her neck. He didn't stop there, but dragged his lips to her earlobe, then to her temple.

"You're tense," he murmured, and used his tongue along the shell of her ear. His hand cupped the front of her shoulder, applying pressure.

"Oh—" Surprised by the unexpected maneuver, she started when he urged her to lie back.

But he was gentle, guiding her down, making sure she landed easily. The towel she'd wrapped around her shoulders fell open, but warm now, she didn't need it. She stared up into his shadowed face, then past him to the dark glittering sky. "I'm amazed we can see so many stars being this close to Waikiki."

"It's even better on the north shore." He drew back, and balanced himself on his elbows, his face turned toward the sky. "No light pollution from high-rises where I live."

She smiled. "You've already sold me. I really do want to go see your place."

"People who come here and stay in Waikiki their whole vacation have not seen Hawaii."

"A woman I worked with told me I needed to go to the other islands. Maui and Kauai, I think?"

He corrected her pronunciation, putting more emphasis on the vowels, then added, "Yep, Kauai especially. Maui's gotten too commercial for my taste, though there are still some awesome places like Haleakala and Hana. Even here on Oahu a lot of spots would blow you away they're so green and beautiful and untouched."

"I've seen pictures."

"Not the same."

The passion in his voice fueled her excitement. "I've always wanted to see a waterfall."

"I know the perfect place. Do you like to hike?" He changed positions to lie on his side, facing her. "The mountains here seem to go on forever," he said, and casually splayed a hand on her belly. "If you're adventurous enough, you can still find places no one's ever been."

It always caught her off guard when he touched her. Her family weren't huggers. Even as a kid she was rarely patted on the head or kissed on the cheek.

"I'm not very athletic," she warned, in case he had some foolish idea they'd go backpacking into the clouds. It looked fun, even romantic on the big screen. And it so wasn't going to happen. Not for her. "I haven't made time to exercise in ages. I'm sure you've already figured that out," she muttered as an aside.

He lifted his head. "How would I know that?" He ran his palm up her belly over her rib cage, stopping just below her breasts. "I'm not getting that impression. Maybe I should explore further." He'd slid his hand beneath the hem of her top before her addled brain could register his intention.

"What are you doing?"

"Really?" he said with a laugh.

"Shut up."

She acknowledged the sudden throb of longing in her chest, resentful of the barriers between them.

She shuddered when his fingers slipped inside a silk cup and grazed the sensitive puckered flesh of her right breast.

He dipped his head, briefly kissed her lips. "Do you want me to make love to you here?" he asked in a low sexy murmur that seemed to dance along her nerve endings. He caressed her nipple, plucking lightly at it until she'd arched her back.

She couldn't answer, couldn't think straight. Not when he pushed her tank top up high enough to expose her bra. He fingered the front clasp but left it fastened, then managed to shove the material aside, baring her left breast. The cool damp air mingled with his warm breath, laving her tingling skin.

The anticipation was too much.

"Yes."

He looked up at her, and while he could surely see her face under the moonlight, she had trouble reading his. She thought he might be smiling, and then he kissed her again, doing all the right things with his teeth and tongue and hot, talented mouth.

Then he stopped and covered her breast with the silk cup. "I am going to make love to you, Lindsey, but you should be relaxed and totally into it. It's not right otherwise. I want you to enjoy every second."

She'd never heard those kinds of words from a man. His tone was warm and reassuring and she was touched that he understood that it wasn't easy for her to loosen up. But the truth was she felt safe with Rick. She could hear it in his voice, had seen it in his eyes that he wanted her.

Before she could even mourn the loss of his hand at her breast, he gently tucked his hand inside her shorts. Shocked, she jerked, but instinctively welcomed his intimate touch as he stroked between her thighs.

"Mmm, you're wet." He pressed slow kisses on her neck and collarbone, distracting her while he slid his fingers under the elastic of her panties.

She tensed again, but focused on the pleasure he was giving her, hastily she kissed him back. It turned into nothing more than a hasty mating of lips, a whimper stolen by the stiff ocean breeze. The second his finger found her clit, the world stopped. Lindsey squeezed her eyes shut, and clutched his arm. It felt like tempered sculpted steel beneath her palm.

"Lie back, Lindsey," he whispered in a husky, yet soothing voice. "Let me take care of you."

With a little smile on her lips, she slumped back in a limp heap. This is what she'd wanted from the moment she thought she might see him again. Only Rick could take care of her better than she could herself. No other man had ever made her come like Rick.

He knew just where to touch her, just how much pressure to use, how to circle his thumb just so. How to bite softly at her lips while his long lean finger penetrated her.

Barely able to breathe, it took her a second to adjust to the sensual invasion. Her muscles clenched his finger, her entire body tensing tighter than a violin string as she surged upward against his hand. And then his thumb moved again, and her shoulders relaxed against the towel and the hard-packed sand as more pleasure shimmered through her body.

She fisted the towel at her sides, opened her eyes to the blur of twinkling stars. She moistened her dry lips, then stilled when he took over the job, sweeping his tongue across her mouth, then pushing inside.

He plunged his finger in deeper, and his thumb swirled the slick wetness around the sensitive nub, the friction growing almost unbearable. Unable to breathe, she tore her mouth away from his. She didn't know how much more she could take...

The first wave hit with alarming force. She whimpered, struggled against succumbing too quickly. But it was too late. She was hot, then cold, then feverish. She was already drowning when the next wave overwhelmed her, pulled her under as her entire body convulsed.

"Lindsey." His voice was a hoarse whisper, and his arms were suddenly around her, holding her tightly against his chest as the tremors continued to shake her.

She buried her face in his shoulder, pressing her lips together, shocked at the tears that had sprung to her eyes. A breath shuddered deep in her chest as the last convulsion claimed her. Drained, she sagged against him, only then feeling the frantic pounding of his heartbeat.

He drew back, touched her face. "What's this?"

Her fingers flew to her damp cheeks. "I don't know," she said, the quiver in her voice making her sound like a liar. "I really don't because that was—" she sighed "—wonderful."

"Good." He hugged her more tightly, shifting so that she was snug against him.

She slid a hand down his flat belly, over the ridges of muscle to the waistband of his shorts. He was fully aroused beneath the fly. She'd barely touched him when she heard his sharp intake of breath.

Gently, he moved her hand away. "Later," he said, and kissed her hair.

She didn't understand. Clearly he was turned on. Although she was still a bit dazed, and so tired she felt as if she'd just run a marathon. Moving to rest her head more comfortably on his shoulder took far more effort than it should have.

"Check out the moon," he said softly. "You can see the contours of the craters."

She looked up, but a passing cloud was in the way. She waited, closing her eyes, listening to the mild lapping of the water, soaking in the stillness of the balmy night, feeling safe and content with Rick's arm curled around her.

The cloud…it had to have passed by now. Yet opening her eyes seemed like too great a chore.

RICK LISTENED UNTIL he heard her breathing change and he knew she'd fallen asleep. Taking care not to disturb her, with his free hand he reached for the extra towel and bunched it behind his head. The moon was in clear view again, and he focused on analyzing each shadow rather than dwell on his erection, or how much he wanted to push up her top and bare her breasts. Steal a taste of those ripe pink nipples.

It didn't help that he had perfect recall of how her nude body had looked in the moonlight the night they'd met. The week of wild parties and too much booze had wound down. Most of the students were booked on flights home the next day, and someone had come up with the idea to have one big bash, post open invitations at all the hotels, get as many people as possible together for a giant farewell to Waikiki.

Feeling like crap two days earlier, he'd already cooled it on the alcohol consumption by then, and being clearheaded and older than the guys he sometimes hung with, he knew hotel management would cut the party short. He went anyway, arriving early to grab a choice getaway spot in case the cops showed up.

Hundreds of students had converged on the pool area that evening, lots of women, a parade of hot bodies. He had a vague recollection of Lindsey's two friends, both pretty, wearing skimpy bikinis like countless others. Lindsey had worn one, too, but she'd been the only hot woman who'd hidden under a knee-length cover-up.

That alone had caught his attention, and then he'd watched her quietly trail her gregarious friends. He knew right off that she was shy and not into the party scene. She smiled and did all the polite things when guys tried hitting on her, but she never initiated conversation, shook her head a lot, blushed even more and never drifted far from her friends.

He'd been working on a strategy to approach her himself when he noticed a herd of hotel security in their distinctive blue shirts headed toward the pool. In minutes everyone would scatter, and he knew he'd lose her if he didn't act fast. Her tall, dark-headed friend had just walked off with some dude toward the beach and the other one looked to be on the verge of a hook-up.

Rick had swooped in and warned Lindsey they were all about to be busted. He'd taken her hand, ready to run with her, when he'd made the mistake of looking into her big blue startled eyes. Like a dumbstruck stupid kid, he'd frozen. Just stood there like a damn chump. He couldn't think, couldn't move, couldn't stop staring. Lindsey was the one who'd squeezed his hand, smiled shyly and suggested they get out of there.

That image of her face had stayed with him for months, years. It was crazy. He'd never been the sentimental type. But when he'd awoken the next morning, alone in the small cove, left with only the impression of her feet in the sand as she'd left him while he slept, he'd gone nuts. He hadn't known her last name, or where she was staying or what school she'd gone to.

Her sweet innocent scent had stayed with him for days, the taste of her lingered for weeks. The soft whimpering sounds she'd made when she came...

The memories made him consider a brisk swim to settle himself down. But he wouldn't risk waking her.

It seemed impossible that she could have stayed so sweet and innocent after all this time. Not untouched, he clearly knew, but surprisingly shy and naive. No, not naive. Inexperienced. A more worldly woman wouldn't blush the way she did, particularly a woman who looked like Lindsey. With that long blond hair, angelic face and wide blue eyes, she could do some serious damage to a man. No way he'd even see it coming.

He gazed down and studied the thick lashes fanning her cheeks, the slight part of her lips. She looked younger than twenty-seven now that he thought about it. Could she have lied about her age? The idea made him uneasy.

Nah. The lie about her name was probably her limit.

He'd been fooled before, though. Nowadays it seemed that half the girls who hung out at Waimea and Sunset were thirteen going on thirty.

Rick was no saint, but he stayed away from women under twenty-one. In fact, he'd found himself pulling away from casual sex more and more. Maybe because hooking up had gotten too easy. There was no fun or challenge anymore, no slow buildup that lit a fire in your belly and got your heart pounding. Hell, that was true of life lately.

The surfboard shop he owned was a reasonable

distraction when he spent time there. The place was finally breaking even, and he liked employing some kids who otherwise might have found less principled means to line their pockets. But the store didn't need his supervision. Wally took care of business. The veteran surfer had stepped in and tightened the reins. Which worked out fine since it allowed Rick more time to work on his new board design.

The wind picked up, and with it a slight chill swept off the ocean. Lindsey stirred, and snuggled closer to him. For him it wasn't cold. He didn't mind the drop in temperature. Most of his winters had been spent in Michigan shoveling snow. He moved his arm so that her cheek rested on his chest, and tried to remember where she'd grown up, or if she'd even told him. Someplace in the Midwest, he was pretty sure. Or maybe he was getting confused because she'd recently lived in Chicago. He'd been there a couple of times in the middle of winter. Not to his liking.

Rick yanked the towel out from under his head, gave it a one-handed shake and spread it over her. He remembered now what Lindsey had told him. She'd moved around a lot as a kid, mostly sticking to the Great Lakes area and Florida, but never staying anywhere more than three years. Something to do with her father's job. Hard to make friends that way.

More clouds had drifted over the beach, blotting out the moon and stars. It was harder for him to see her. But her body was warm and snug against his, and for now that was enough.

5

VOICES BROKE INTO her crazy dream about Easter bunnies and surfboards. Was someone talking to her? No, the voices were distant. Easter bunnies? Where had that come from?

Lindsey flexed her left shoulder, and tried to straighten out her arm. Something was in her way. Still groggy, she slowly rolled onto her back, wiggling to lose the lumpy blanket under her shoulder blade. Frustrated that she couldn't get comfy, she opened her eyes.

This wasn't her room.

She stared up at the muted gray sky.

Her heart jumped, and then she remembered. They'd had a picnic on the beach, and she'd dozed. But hadn't it been dark already?

She turned her head and faced Rick just as he opened his eyes, a slow lazy smile lifting the corners of his mouth. The lumpy blanket turned out to be his arm, which he curled around her.

"Mornin'," he murmured and pulled her toward him.

"Good morning." She smiled back, briefly closing

her eyes when his ill-aimed kiss landed half on her cheek and partly on her eyelid. A second later his words sunk in. "Morning? No, it can't be." She pushed away, scrambled to a sitting position and scanned the hazy gray horizon.

Coming from behind, there were voices, too distant to be distinct. She remembered now. That's what had awoken her.

She glanced over her shoulder and saw two men carrying surfboards under their arms, still a good way down the beach but headed toward them.

"Is it really morning?" she asked, panicked.

Rick unhurriedly sat up and squinted at the water. "Nice swells."

"Oh, my God." She rubbed her gritty eyes. How could she have been so stupid, so inconsiderate? Mia and Shelby had probably contacted search-and-rescue by now. She had to get back to the hotel, call them, let them know she was all right.

"I must've dozed off after you." He arched backward, stretching out his arms.

"I have to—" She broke off, and stared at the breadth of his shoulders and chest, at the definition of muscle along his forearms, the bunching of his biceps before they disappeared under the T-shirt sleeve. The man had been carved out of bronze, and no one could convince her otherwise.

"I'm sorry, Jill, what did—" He stopped, stricken for a second, and then gave her a wry grin. "Hey, you've been Jill in my head for six years. I get a pass until Lindsey sticks."

Unsettled, she tugged at the hem of her shirt. He'd

been thinking of her for six years? No, in the light of day the idea was absurd. She couldn't have made that big of an impression on him, not even as the adventurous Jill. A man like Rick probably had more women interested in him than he knew what to do with.

Naturally Lindsey had thought about him over the years. In the beginning, after she'd returned to NYU to finish her senior year, a night hadn't gone by without her reliving those hours on the beach. The obsession only stopped because she'd feared she would flunk every one of her finals if she didn't get more sleep. But then, she'd never had an orgasm before Rick.

She cleared her throat. "I forgot what we were saying."

He agilely got to his feet, extended her a hand. "I have an idea."

She let him pull her up while she fixated on his long lean fingers, remembering where they'd been last night. Oh, God. She felt warm suddenly. Not a blush, or maybe it was, but this time her whole body was involved. The sense memory of convulsing at his touch had her squeezing her thighs together.

Her nipples tightened, and he obviously knew it. He was staring at them.

"Someone's coming," she said, and bent to scoop up one of the towels.

"Just a couple of surfers."

"We should go."

"Yep." He picked up the mat and rolled it up.

"My friends are going to kill me."

"Why? You texted them last night."

She could hear the voices coming closer, and her

anxiety level rose. It wasn't as if she and Rick had been caught doing anything wrong. "I told them we were eating on the beach, not that I was staying out all night," she said.

He grinned. "I bet they figured it out."

She rolled her eyes and grabbed the other towel, hastily folding it in half. She hated the sudden awkwardness that came over her. A shrink would probably blame her parents. Sometimes she did, too. Except both her brothers had grown up in the same oppressively strict, never-say-the-word-*sex* household as she had, and they didn't seem to have problems expressing themselves.

In fact, her older brother, Brian, had rebelled in the opposite direction. He'd become a father at seventeen. Lindsey had been more astonished than her puritanical parents. She'd been almost eighteen before she even kissed a boy.

Looking past her at the strangers, Rick smiled and lifted his chin in greeting. He said something about the waves she didn't understand, but the two men apparently did since they responded in kind.

Courtesy dictated that she at least acknowledge them. She turned, saw that they were older teenagers who were walking along the water's edge. She smiled, but they didn't seem to notice her. The lanky blond boy stared openly at Rick, and even in the shadowy dawn light, she could see admiration on his face.

"Hey," he said, "I saw you out there in December when Sunset was breaking at thirteen."

The shorter, stockier boy grinned, his teeth white against his dark round face. "You were awesome, dude." He flashed him a hand sign using his extended thumb and little finger. "When are we gonna see you at the Triple Crown?"

Rick shrugged. "Maybe next year."

"C'mon, brah, you said that last February in Surfer," the shorter one said, pausing for Rick's response.

The taller boy kept walking. "Let's go, Skeet." He gestured with a nod to Rick. "See ya, dude."

"You guys have a good one," Rick said, and started draining the cooler.

Lindsey sensed that the second boy had finally moved on, but her gaze was on Rick. "Do you know them?"

He shook his head. "The colas are still cold. Want one?" He popped open a can. "At least until we can get some coffee."

"Thanks." She took a sip, her dry icky mouth feeling instantly better. "Sorry, I don't have time for coffee."

He'd opened a can for himself, did a visual sweep of the area, then balanced the soda on top of the cooler. "We have to hurry."

Quickly, she gathered the mat and towels, while he hefted the cooler. Glad as she was that he understood her need to return to the hotel, she was a bit annoyed with his sudden rush to be rid of her.

She followed him, finding the sand more difficult to walk in than she had last night, but seriously glad her lagging allowed her to shove a couple of old mints from her purse into her mouth. They didn't speak until they got to the Jeep, and he'd thrown everything in a messy heap in the back.

After they'd both climbed in, he quickly buckled himself up, waited for her to get settled and said, "Ready?" at the same time he started to reverse.

"I guess I'd better be."

His gaze flicked to her, and he smiled. "We're probably too late but it's worth a try."

"Too late for what?" she asked, and grabbed the dashboard when he rolled through a stop sign and accelerated onto the highway, heading away from Waikiki. "Uh, the hotel is in the other direction."

"We'll get there eventually."

"No, Rick, my friends, you don't understand—"

"You go back this early you'll only wake them up. Text them. If they're worried because you aren't back yet, they'll check their phones."

She considered his argument, then dug out her phone. Mia and Shelby were going to think she'd lost her mind. No messages. They obviously weren't too worried. "So where are we going?"

"To catch the sunrise."

"Wouldn't that be on the other side of the island?"

"It is."

The sky had begun to lighten before they'd left the beach. "We're too late," she said.

"It's still dawn. The sun won't come up off the water for another half hour."

She thought for a minute. "I guess they are separate events."

Rick smiled. "Ever see a sunrise, a real sunrise?"

"I'm not usually up that early," she said dryly. "No, I take that back." Lindsey had a flash of memory that hadn't surfaced in years. "I was young, maybe eight or nine. My family had just moved to Florida, and we were staying in a motel until my mom found a house to rent." She sighed. "Boy, did I get a whipping that day."

"Why?" He briefly took his gaze from the road and shot her a troubled look.

"So did my brothers," she said defensively, wishing she'd kept her mouth shut. It was embarrassing to think about how quick her father was to get out his belt. "None of us had seen the ocean before and—" She shrugged. "The point is, I did get to see the sun rising over the water. It was amazing. I can't believe I forgot that until now."

Rick was quiet for a long uncomfortable stretch, then he said, "I can't see you as a problem child."

"Me? Are you kidding? I was Saint Lindsey. My older brother still calls me that sometimes."

"Did you get hit often?"

"No." She hated that he would have a misguided impression of her childhood. "Only one other time, and no surprise, I was being disciplined for an incident that involved my brothers." Normally she wouldn't elaborate on something so personal, but when she saw disbelief in the grim set of his jaw, she added, "My parents were both very strict. I abided by their rules, did what they expected of me so I was fine. My brothers not so much."

"Define strict."

She took a deep breath. "Well, they didn't send me to boarding school, or anything like that. Although that wouldn't have been too tragic," she added absently. "At least I would've gotten to stay in one place."

"I remember you saying that you'd moved around a lot. That's gotta be tough on a kid," he said, reaching over to rub her thigh.

She laid her hand on top of his, amazed at how much

longer his fingers were. "It's hard to make friends. I ended up staying home and studying a lot."

"What about dating? The boys must have been pounding down your front door."

Lindsey snorted. "Sure. I had them taking numbers."

They came up on a sharp curve, and he moved his hand to down shift. "Come on, admit it. You left a trail of broken hearts after every move."

"Ah, you're sweet," she said with a laugh, and lightly stroked his cheek. The rough feel of his unshaven jaw made the tips of her fingers tingle.

"Sweet? Hell, I'm serious." He looked at her, but was forced to return his attention to the tricky twists in the road.

"I was always quiet and shy, definitely not the cheerleader type. Much more studious." She wanted to touch him again, wanted him to touch her, but she understood that he needed to concentrate on his driving. "It didn't matter. I doubt my father would have allowed me to date."

"When?"

"Ever." She laughed. "I'm exaggerating. I had two dates during my senior year."

Rick frowned. "That's it?"

"It was no big deal. Really, I was—" She cut herself short, wisely nipping the admission that she'd been half-afraid of boys. Partly the fault of her parents, but her brothers' relentless teasing had something to do with her having believed the worst of the opposite sex. "I had a perfectly fine childhood."

He slid her a speculative look, and then shook his head. "I'm not judging."

"Um, yes, you are. But it's okay. I suppose we all judge to some degree when faced with an experience different from our own."

A conciliatory smile curved his mouth. "I thought you were an accountant."

"And an armchair psychiatrist when I see an opening."

He chuckled. "Good to know. I'll watch myself."

She smiled wryly. "Guess I should've reserved that comment until after I got the scoop on your family."

"Hey, I'm an open book."

She waited expectantly, her patience soon slipping. "Well?"

He lifted a shoulder. "We're a typical, boring family. I have two older brothers, a sister who is younger than me. My dad is a pharmacist, my mom works part-time at my nieces and nephews' elementary school."

"Do you all get along?"

"Pretty much, except when it comes to football. My idiot brothers like the Cowboys."

Lindsey laughed.

Rick cocked a brow at her. "Don't tell me you're a Cowboys fan."

"I've never thought about it."

He gave her an exaggerated look of surprise. "Not a football fan?"

"Is that a deal breaker?"

He pretended to give the matter serious thought. "We're coming up on baseball season. I can forgive and forget."

Her inflated sigh of relief earned her a smile that could've melted butter, and when she sighed again, it was a whisper-soft sound muffled by the engine, meant with all her heart.

She'd be gone before the season even started.

The irritating thought came out of nowhere and was quickly squashed. This was only her second day in Hawaii. That kind of musing wasn't allowed. Her gaze drifted to his hands, to the long tan fingers wrapped around the steering wheel. He was busy navigating the turns in the road, and she treated herself to an uninterrupted sizing-up of his windblown hair, his strong profile, the way his thigh muscles flexed when he put in the clutch. Even in the dim light of dawn he took her breath away.

Her mind drew back to that long-ago night, and she wondered why he'd singled her out. This wasn't the first time she'd reflected on the puzzle. There had been well over a hundred women at the pool, most of them wearing teeny tiny bikinis. Either braver or drunker than the rest, a few of the women had jumped into the pool and tossed their tops onto the deck.

Even Mia and Shelby had gotten into the spirit of the week and splurged on thong bikinis. Next to them, practically swimming in her oversized white cover-up, Lindsey had looked like their den mother. Yet when hotel security had forced everyone to scatter, she'd been the one who Rick had whisked away, dragging her along the beach, laughing and running until she couldn't breathe.

"Damn, this stop is going to cost us," he said, applying the brakes.

She whipped her gaze to the road and saw that the light had turned red at the intersection.

He shifted gears, and twisted around to face her. He leaned in, resting his arm on the back of her seat, and kissed her shoulder. The light rasp of his stubbly chin against her skin made her quiver.

When he gazed at her, she caught a whiff of his minty breath and smiled.

"What's that for?"

"What?"

"This," he said, and traced the outline of her lips with the tip of his forefinger. "So soft and innocent," he murmured, and briefly pressed a tender kiss to her mouth.

Her eyes fluttered closed, and then abruptly opened when his words sunk in. "Innocent?"

He stole another quick kiss and winked. "How can you look this good first thing in the morning?"

Ha, she couldn't imagine what a wreck she was. Why hadn't she pulled herself together before the sky had started getting light? She finger-combed her hair, and flipped down the visor, praying for a mirror so she could dab away the inevitable black smudges under her eyes.

He caught her chin, and brought her face back to his. He stared into her eyes for an endless moment, then lowered his gaze to her mouth. "You're perfect," he said. "Don't change a thing."

She gave a nervous laugh, and swatted away his hand. "Innocent," she said, in case he thought she'd forgotten the absurd remark. "Right."

Rick returned his hands to the wheel. "Would that be a crime?"

"No, but you of all people know better," she said quietly, the heat rushing to her face.

She wasn't sorry for what had happened the night they met, but she had wondered what he thought of a woman who'd have sex with him only four hours after meeting him. It didn't matter that so many people her age seemed to place little importance on casual hookups. What she'd done had been completely out of character. Now that she'd given him a hint of her upbringing, she couldn't imagine what he was thinking. That she'd rebelled and slept with every guy she met? Oh, God, she'd basically sent out a booty call on Facebook.

She stared straight ahead, saw the light turn green, felt the Jeep jerk into gear. She wanted to look at him… no, she couldn't. Not now.

But when he steered the Jeep to the shoulder of the road and cut the engine, she turned her head to meet his warm concerned eyes.

He said nothing, only cupped a hand behind her neck and drew her close. His mouth touched hers. With firm, closed lips, he grazed the corners of her mouth, slanted his head and pressed harder. Then he let her go, just when she wanted more.

She stared at him as he got them back on the highway. He seemed pleased with himself, pleased with the whole situation, and she had to wonder about that. She'd put herself in this man's hands. Sensible, responsible Lindsey was in a car, headed who knew where, with a veritable stranger and she felt completely safe. What was it about him that made her bend all her rules? She'd have said it was out of character again, but that excuse only worked once. She'd planned this. Hoped for it, dreamt of it. Perhaps her assumptions about her character needed a fresh look.

She leaned back in her seat, her smile as pleased as Rick's.

6

BY THE TIME THEY made it past Sandy Beach, the sun had risen above the water. There were residual beams of red and gold streaking the sky, but Rick's favorite time had passed. No sweat. There was always tomorrow.

Anyway, he was distracted. Lindsey had given him a lot to think about. He was beginning to understand the reason for her lack of experience. The bit about her father whipping her left a sour taste in his mouth. Bad enough striking a kid, but a little girl? Hard to get past that one. Had anyone, including his father, laid a hand on his sister, Rick would've had him by the throat.

He pulled the Jeep into the last lookout before Sea Life Park, and killed the engine. "We missed it," he said, shrugging.

"I somehow got that impression." Lindsey grinned, and focused on a couple of bodysurfers who were taking advantage of the moderate swells. "It's still beautiful. What was that last beach we passed? There were a whole bunch of kids in the water. Is today a local holiday?"

"No, but kids here always seem to find time to sneak off to the beach before or after school, especially if the waves are hitting over five feet. Sandy breaks near shore which is good for bodysurfers and boogie boarders. On weekends the place is packed."

"Do you bodysurf, too?"

Rick looked at her and laughed. "No."

She wrinkled her nose. "Why is that funny?"

He wasn't insulted because she didn't understand the sport or culture. "Let's see, how can I explain it?" He considered it for a few seconds, and then, controlling a smile, he took her small soft hand and pressed it between his palms. "Okay, pretend we've just met. I like you, you like me, we're walking along the beach and I take your hand. It's kind of like testing the water, maybe wading up to your waist, splashing around, whatever."

"Okay," she drawled, her brows arched in amusement.

He linked their fingers, their palms meeting. He regretted his was scratchy from working on his new board design, but she didn't seem to mind. "Say we walk for half an hour, talking, and we're starting to like each other more. We stop and I put my arms around you." The gearshift was in the way. "Wanna get out of the car for a better look at the bay?"

"Sure." She frowned a little. "But what does this have to do—?"

"Ah." He held up a finger. "Don't be impatient," he said and climbed out of the Jeep.

Her lips pursed, she slipped out of the passenger side, and warily met him where he waited, leaning against the hood, his legs spread.

He pulled her close and looped his hands around her waist. She tilted her head back to look up at him, and he felt the quickening of her heart against his chest, echoing his own. "This feels nice. Agreed?"

She slowly nodded, a smile twitching at the corners of her mouth. "I thought we were going to get a better look."

"We will, but I'm trying to give you an analogy here," he said with a straight face. "Okay, at this point we've decided to get our hair wet, swim a few laps." He lowered his head, allowed his mouth to lightly brush hers, lifted and then settled again more firmly. He moved his head, just enough to assert more pressure and coax an opening. She trembled a little, which only made him impatient to sample more than her lips, but he stuck to the lesson plan.

With the tip of his tongue he teased and tasted until he knew she was ready, and then slid his tongue inside, slowly, making a thorough sweep, showing her how much he wanted her, yet letting her know that they were just getting started.

Before he got ahead of himself, he stopped and set her at arm's length.

She gazed up at him with wide startled eyes, her lips damp from his mouth. "What's next?" she asked in a breathy voice.

"We like swimming. It's fun, but the waves have kicked up and we see some other people bodysurfing," he said, his own voice huskier. "And we think, hey, that looks like fun." He shot a look down Kalanianaole Highway. So far no cars had sped by them but they were still too much out in the open. "Come here," he said, taking her hand and leading her to an outcropping of black lava rock.

He found a portion of the cliff that wouldn't scratch

the hell out of his back yet still offered a modicum of privacy. Below them about fifty feet, the waves crashed against the rocks. She glanced down, but didn't seem bothered by the height or the turbulent water. He positioned them a safe distance from the edge, his back to the rock wall.

"The swimming was nice, and in fact, we'll do more of that," he said, trying to keep a straight face when she looked at him as if he'd been underwater too long, his brain deprived of oxygen. "But it's time to try bodysurfing. You with me?"

"You're crazy. You do know that, right?"

Grinning, he found the hem of her tank top and slid both hands beneath the fabric.

She jerked back, glanced over her shoulder, tried halfheartedly to push him away.

"We're fine." He cupped both breasts, easily zeroing in on her already hard nipples through the bra. "Hmm, we like bodysurfing," he said, sliding his fingers inside the silky cups.

Lindsey let out a shaky laugh. "You're seconds away from a straitjacket."

He rubbed his thumb across the hot beaded flesh, his body tightening with need. "Bummer, that would seriously put a kink on bodysurfing."

"Rick, we shouldn't—" Her lashes briefly lowered, and she made a soft whimpering sound as she moved against his fingers.

He pushed up her top, slid the cup aside and took her nipple into his mouth. He suckled deeply, nibbled lightly and then rolled his tongue over the rosy nub. She tensed, then murmured something about a car coming.

He'd checked. They were in the clear, especially with the Jeep shielding them from passing traffic.

But he cooled it anyway, forced himself to tear his mouth away. He'd gotten uncomfortably hard and it was going to be one hell of a long ride back to her hotel. Digging deep for willpower, he pulled her tank top back down. And stared into her dazed eyes. Down at her soft innocent mouth.

Guilt flared inside him. Dammit. No reason to feel guilty just because he'd been given a part of the puzzle. So she'd had a strict upbringing. Lindsey had certainly learned all she needed to know about sex along the way. She was a grown woman. She'd put the call out to him on Facebook. Lindsey was no virgin and she hadn't contacted him to take her sightseeing.

Still, he'd come on pretty strong. He'd gone straight for the sweet spot. She wasn't that type of woman. He shook his head at the notion, but it was true. Lindsey was different. He really liked that about her. Not the kind of like that lasted only a couple of nights. She deserved more than being felt up on the side of the highway.

"What's wrong?" she asked, touching his waist.

"I'm hungry." He adjusted her tank top, and refused to look at her hard nipples poking at the stretchy material. "Let's go get breakfast. Then I'll take you back to the hotel."

She nervously moistened her lips. "What about…our lesson?"

He shook his head. "It was a dumb idea."

As tempting as the macadamia-nut, chocolate-chip pancakes were, Lindsey could barely eat. Rick had no such trouble. After wolfing down his ham-and-cheese omelet and fried potatoes, he put away two of her left-over pancakes. She hoped his appetite was a sign that nothing was bothering him, but his earlier abruptness had her on edge.

The three cups of strong black Kona coffee certainly hadn't helped her nerves. God, she was ridiculous. Hcrc she was lucky enough to be in Hawaii, while March snow was forecasted for Chicago, sitting under a palm tree at an outdoor café with the most gorgeous man this side of the equator.

And still, she found something to fret about. Such a pathetic Lindsey thing to do. Maybe that was the problem. He was tired of her. Maybe he'd figured out that the woman he knew as Jill didn't exist.

"Have your friends texted you back yet?" he asked, and signaled the waitress for the check.

Lindsey got her phone out of her purse at the same time she took out her wallet. "No, but it doesn't matter. Just drop me off at the hotel."

He paused in the middle of pushing his plate aside. Frowning, he met her eyes. "Drop you off?"

She looked away. "I'm sure you have other things to do today," she said, sounding deceptively unconcerned.

"I thought you were coming to the North Shore with me."

The waitress interrupted them by bringing the check. Lindsey reached for it, but Rick was too fast.

"It's my turn," she stubbornly reminded him.

He ignored her, and after a quick glance at the total, returned the check to the waitress along with some folded bills. "Keep the change," he told the woman, and then said to Lindsey, "You ready?"

Once out of the booth, she was surprised when he took her hand. He silently led her out of the restaurant, to the passenger side of the Jeep, and opened the door for her.

When he got in, he didn't start the engine. Instead, he put on his sunglasses and turned to her. "I understand that you're only here for a week," he said. "You probably have other plans with your friends."

"Not really," she said slowly, not sure where he was going with this. "It's just that we haven't talked much yet."

"Look, I'll admit it. I'm a selfish bastard. I was hoping we'd have the whole week together. If I've been too pushy, I apologize."

"No," she said, pleased by his honesty and that she'd worried for nothing. "You haven't."

"It's not about sex, either. Naturally, I wouldn't turn it down." He shrugged and smiled, when she gave him an arched look. "I'm just saying..."

She silently congratulated herself for not blushing or flinching. "Saying what exactly?" she asked calmly, reminding herself that she was the warrior, Jill. "That if I open the door, you'll walk in and help yourself?"

His brows went up in surprise, and he chuckled. "Yeah, pretty much."

"Okay, then."

"Okay, what?" He leaned back, looking totally relaxed, peering at her through the dark lenses.

"What I'm hearing is that you're letting me call the shots."

He hesitated. "Go on."

She couldn't see his eyes, of course, but she heard the amusement in his voice, saw a smile tugging at the corners of his mouth. "First, I have to stop someplace where I can buy a pair of sunglasses. Then I want to go back to the hotel and shower." She paused, enjoying the slight tensing of his jaw, the hopeful way his brows arched. "Alone," she said, and when his lips puckered with disappointment, she stupidly added, "Sorry."

Darn it. She didn't have to apologize. She was in charge. No, she was *taking* charge. Just like Jill would do. Or Mia, or Shelby. But she wouldn't beat herself up. She had to accept that the new Lindsey was a work in progress. Shedding her old skin couldn't happen overnight. She'd already taken the important step of quitting her job and leaving her old boring life behind. This wasn't simply a new chapter, but a new beginning.

She squared her shoulders. "I do have to find out what's going on with my friends, but I also want to go to the North Shore with you."

"I should've said something sooner, but they're welcome to come along."

She had to smile at his obvious lack of enthusiasm. Though she understood. She loved them both to pieces, but she didn't particularly want to share Rick with them. Besides, she figured they were having reunions of their own.

As if he'd read her mind, he said, "I'm guessing they've found better things to do than hang with us."

"One would hope. This week is going to go by fast enough."

"Yep." He started the engine. "Store first, then the hotel."

"No." Lindsey shook her head and leaned toward him. "First this." She braced her hand on his hard thigh, and kissed him on the mouth.

He didn't move. Didn't try to intensify the kiss when she kept it light. In fact, she got the impression that he wanted her to have complete control. And to her amazement, she had the feeling she could really get used to that.

RICK WAITED IN THE Jeep while Lindsey ran in to the nearby ABC store to find a pair of sunglasses. He'd offered to go in with her, but she'd flatly refused. Hell, not just refused, she'd ordered him to stay in the car, and punctuated it with a glare that said she meant it.

He smiled at her fierce new assertiveness. She would probably be disappointed to know that while she was talking like a general, her eyes were practically blinking out an SOS. He wouldn't tell her, though, because that was a huge part of what made her so great. Her emotions were written all over her face, everything from pleasure to fear to the fantastic way her eyes widened when she surprised herself. Maybe that's why she wanted the sunglasses.

He didn't care. She had other tells. Like the way she wrinkled her nose when she was confused or uncertain, or how she pressed her lips together when she regretted giving up too much information. But he was still learning to read her. That first night had been spent mainly in the dark, talking, touching. Yeah, a lot of touching.

The whole evening had been crazy. He'd been full of

pent-up energy after spending a restless day contemplating whether he was doing the right thing by staying in school. He'd been a month short of twenty-three, and because he'd started college at twenty, he was still a sophomore.

That meant three more years of school in order to get his engineering degree. He hadn't been sure he was on the right path. As much as he got off on learning how things worked and being able to create something from nothing, the thought of an office job filled him with dread.

Walking away from school wouldn't have been hard. He hadn't needed an education to secure his future. As long as he didn't get stupid with the money he'd invested, he'd be able to live the rest of his life on a beach somewhere and not lift a finger. At twenty-three, the idea had been damn tempting. Until he'd spent that night with Lindsey.

She may have been insecure about spring-break sex, but man, she'd been sure as hell about her future.

She wasn't going to school for her parents or because it was expected of her. She'd told him that she wanted as many options as possible. That's what her degree was about—options. She didn't want to wake up one day filled with regret, unable to change the past.

At the time, he'd had too many options. At eighteen, he'd earned serious cash as an oil rig diver, and somehow he'd come up with a simple fix for an endemic problem with high pressure valves. With his patent, money ceased to be an issue. Wouldn't be, in fact, for the rest of his life. He could kick back, surf and ski and travel to his heart's content, but he didn't want one moment of success at twenty to be the apex of his life.

He swore then that he wouldn't let his success change his goals. Except he had. Everyone fussed over his potential, pushed him to start college as he'd promised. As expectations mounted, so had his fear. What if he never had another bankable idea again?

Then he'd met steady, sensible Lindsey and he'd promised himself he'd finish school just as he'd set out to do. Whether he used the degree for a job or not was immaterial. He wouldn't regret having the knowledge. The invention bug had bitten though—he wanted to be that person who could look at anything and know that he could make it something better. He wanted the challenge and he wanted the thrill of success again.

Safety and security had been Lindsey's brass ring. He hadn't totally gotten it at the time, but knowing about her childhood, now he understood. All he knew was that she was sure and steady and more centered than anyone he knew, and he envied her. Because she would never be a woman who would end up disappointed in herself.

He wanted to be that person. Every time he'd been tempted to kiss off school after that night, he thought of her.

Squinting up at the sky, he noticed the clouds were starting to come in from the northeast. Damn, he hoped it didn't rain. March could be an iffy month. Unfortunately, this side of the island could be clear while it rained where he lived. But the rain was what kept the north and windward side lush and green. He had to get her out there. It was a different world, the polar opposite of Waikiki. She was going to love it.

Oddly, it mattered to him that she did. Which made no sense, he thought as he watched an Asian couple take pictures of each other in front of the ABC window display of Hawaiian shirts and colorful rubber flip-flops. In fact, the idea bothered him. What difference should it make to him if she liked the North Shore? In a week she'd be gone.

Lindsey walked out of the store, clutching a bag, her new sunglasses already in place shielding her eyes. He smiled at the bag, thinking that she might have bought one of the many souvenirs hawked by the touristy convenience store that was a Waikiki staple. He was an impatient shopper, in the habit of dashing into stores and grabbing only the thing he needed, but he'd like to watch her shop, he decided. He guessed that she'd be slow and thoughtful, making a mental list of pros and cons as she deliberated over each item.

A shirtless dude riding a bike braked in front of her, and she stopped when he said something to her. Whatever it was, she smiled shyly, shook her head, her shoulder-length blond hair shimmering in the noon sun. The guy eyed her long after she walked away from him, staring admiringly at her from over his aviator-style dark lenses.

Hell, Rick totally understood. He'd have given her a third look. And that was another thing he liked about her. She had a head-turning body, great hair, perfect face and she took it all in stride. Maybe her strict upbringing had something to do with keeping her centered. Whatever, she sure had her act together.

He'd forgotten that he dropped her off in front of the entrance and then found a shady place to park. He only remembered when he saw her hesitate at the curb and look around as if she were confused, and he flagged her down.

She smiled as she climbed into the Jeep. "Interesting store," she said. "I'm going to have to go back and pick up a few things for my family before I leave."

"I'm sure you've noticed that there's one on just about every corner in Waikiki. Thirty-seven of them within a one-mile radius to be exact. Another twenty-seven around Honolulu and on the other islands."

She laughed. "What did you do, drive around and count them?"

"Nope." Rick started the engine. "I tried to buy stock."

7

LINDSEY HAD CALLED both Mia and Shelby right up to the time she and Rick reached the hotel lobby. She'd even tried calling both rooms directly. If they were there, they weren't answering. Though she doubted they'd be wasting such a beautiful day in the room. Shelby had texted something about Mia seeing the guy she'd met during spring break at the bar. Maybe they'd found each other again. Still, she didn't want to take Rick to the room and risk having anyone walk in on them.

They got to the elevator, and she pressed the call button, her mind skipping around for a way she could explain that she needed some privacy without him thinking she was ditching him. It looked as if she were going to have to just spit it out. She took a deep breath and glanced over at him.

He smiled. "I'm not going up with you."

"You're not?"

He removed his sunglasses and hung them off the neckline of his shirt. "Go get your shower, talk to your friends." He touched her hair. "Take your time, Lindsey. I'm not going anywhere."

"What are you going to do?"

"Get a room, if they have one available. If not, I'll try the hotel across the street."

For a horrifying instant she thought he'd given up on taking her to his place. "I thought we were going to the North Shore."

"We are, but it's a two-hour round-trip, so it makes sense for me to have a room here." He rubbed his shadowed jaw. "I can shave, shower, keep a change of clothes for when we're in Waikiki."

"I hate for you to spend the money," she said, knowing that he was trying to make things easier for her. "But with the three of us sharing two rooms, I can't really—"

"I know." He nudged her chin up and brushed a kiss across her lips. "We'll meet at the pool when you're ready. You have my number."

She nodded, and heard the elevator ding. "I'll be at least an hour." She took a step backward, then moved aside for a family to enter the car, without breaking eye contact with him.

It was silly. They were only going to be apart for an hour or two, but she already hated the thought. She boarded the elevator last, then turned to face the lobby. He was still standing there watching her as the doors slid closed. At the last second he winked, and her stupid heart fluttered like a nervous butterfly.

This was amazing. *He* was amazing. Last week she'd harbored a cautious hope that he'd somehow magically show up. At every turn she'd warned herself against disappointment. The chances were slim that he'd have the opportunity, much less want to see her again. But this was so much better than she had imagined.

"What floor?"

Lindsey blinked at the scowling teenage girl with the dyed pink stripe through her hair. From the tone of her voice, the question had been asked more than once.

"Seven. Thanks." Lindsey ignored the other two kids giggling behind her and let herself daydream about Rick.

There was so much more she still had to learn about him. Like how he had the money to invest in stocks. No, her curiosity wasn't about him having the discretionary funds as much as it was about his ambition to invest. He was only twenty-nine, no steady job and obviously no steady paycheck. Yet he carried a lot of cash and didn't seem reluctant to spend it. Which made her think inheritance, but the way he'd described his family, she didn't think so.

She'd done well financially, especially for someone her age, and that was the only reason she felt comfortable enough taking a risk on the new business with Mia and Shelby. But she'd scrimped a lot to build her small nest egg, and she sure never had enough to gamble on the stock market. She hoped he wasn't trying to impress her.

A few seconds of consideration and she rejected the idea. He wasn't the type. Besides, he had enough going for him that he didn't have to pad his appeal.

The elevator stopped at her floor, and as she headed toward the rooms there were no Do Not Disturb signs hanging from either of the doorknobs. She got out her key card and let herself in, already dreading having to look in the mirror.

Once she was inside and saw that the connecting door was open, she called out. It didn't appear that Mia or Shelby was there.

She had mixed feelings about not being able to talk to them. While she wanted to assure herself that they were busy having fun, she wasn't quite ready to talk about Rick. They'd want details she wasn't willing to share.

After dropping her purse and the bag with the self-tanning lotion on the console table, she went straight for the shower. As she stripped, her thoughts, of course, went back to Rick. Understandable, except that her curse in life was to overanalyze everything. Didn't seem to matter that she'd sworn up and down that this trip would be a nonthinking, hedonistic vacation.

Sighing, she leaned into the stall and adjusted the shower spray, proud of herself for resisting the urge to look in the mirror. If she did, she knew full well she'd fixate on every single flaw, real or imagined. For once Lindsey would not allow her worst enemy to win.

HIS HAIR STILL WET, a towel wrapped around his hips, Rick tore the price tags off the two new T-shirts and red swim trunks he'd bought at the ABC store across the street. If he ended up spending the night in Waikiki, he'd have to buy another pair of shorts, but he hoped it worked out that they could take off later for his place. The important thing was not to rush Lindsey.

For the third time since he'd checked in to the hotel an hour ago, his phone beeped. He knew what it was, someone texting or tweeting that surf was up at Waimea, but he checked anyway, in case it was Wally. Rick had left a message for him at In Motion, checking to make sure everything was okay at the shop in case he didn't make it out there tonight.

Rick checked his emails, laughed at the stupid joke his ten-year-old nephew had sent him and then cursed at the price increase his polyurethane supplier was implementing in time for summer surfboard demand. The guy was a shark. No reason the cost should be going up, other than the fact he could get away with it. It really sucked because Rick wouldn't pass on the added cost to his customers. Too many of them were local kids who busted their boards or had them jacked, and couldn't afford to replace them.

As it was he had more employees than the shop warranted. He rarely turned down a poor kid who earnestly wanted their own board. But he never gave anything away. He made them work around the store to pay off the cost. His financial planner had called him three kinds of crazy, but he shrugged it off. As long as the store supported itself—and didn't suck him dry—and his surfing prize money paid the rest of the bills, Rick didn't care.

He set the phone aside, frowning, wondering if he should try the shop again. Odd, no one had answered. Before he could hit speed dial, the mellow sound of Jackson Browne signaled it was Wally. He picked up the phone, surprised at his irritation that it wasn't Lindsey. He'd have to give her her own ring tone. Nothing immediately came to mind. Trying to decide on one that fit her was going to be interesting.

"Where are you?" Wally jumped in when Rick had hesitated, too busy thinking about Lindsey.

"Anything wrong?"

"Waimia's up."

"I heard."

"Everybody's asking where you are."

Rick walked over to the sliding doors leading to the balcony and stared through the glass at the small Waikiki swells. Great for swimming, useless for surfing. "Did you get my message?"

"I got it. You didn't come home last night, either," Wally said, his coarse voice as rusty as an old nail. He looked mean with his long wiry gray hair and the unkempt salt-and-pepper beard, but anyone interested soon learned that the man had a heart of gold.

Rick didn't know how he could run the shop without him. "Everything okay?"

"Skip and Kai were supposed to clean the back room today. Guess who didn't show up? Wait 'til they need a few bucks for smokes."

Rick shook his head. Wally was the worst offender in overindulging the kids. At least Rick wouldn't contribute a penny toward cigarettes and made them work for anything else they wanted from the shop. "Look, I'm trying to get back over to that side by dark, but I don't know yet."

"Back over... Where the hell are you?"

"Waikiki," Rick admitted. He'd said nothing to anyone yesterday because he didn't know how the week would play out with Lindsey. "A friend came in from the mainland. I'm bringing her out this evening or tomorrow."

"To your place?"

"Yeah, to my place," Rick said, hearing the dread in Wally's tone. "Why?"

"Shit."

Rick grabbed a handful of hair at his nape in frustration. This wasn't going to be good. "What do you mean, 'shit'?"

"I let Scooter and Reno crash there last night."

He gritted his teeth. Of all the kids who needed a place to stay last night, why them? "Were they messed up?"

"Only Scooter. Not too bad, though. They brought the key back this morning."

"Okay," Rick said, his mind working fast. This was his own damn fault. He should've warned Wally he could be bringing someone back and his place was temporarily off-limits. "Is anyone still around?"

"Only Deanna."

"Tell her she can apply the time toward working at the shop for her new board, but I need the place cleaned up within four hours."

"Done, brah. Even if I have to do it myself."

Rick snorted. That meant stuffing dirty dishes and towels in closets. "You worry about the shop. If you can't find Deanna, ask Malia or Jonny. I'll check with you later."

He disconnected the call, knowing he could count on his friend to make sure there'd be no unpleasant surprises by the time Rick got back with Lindsey. Wally had spent twenty years in the navy, ten of them stationed on and off in Honolulu. He loved the islands as much as anyone could. The day after he'd been eligible for his pension, he said aloha to Uncle Sam, moved to the

North Shore and hadn't stepped foot off the island for over eighteen years.

Checking his watch, Rick saw that it had been an hour and a half since he saw Lindsey. He grabbed the new trunks and yanked the towel off from around his hips on his way to the bathroom. The contents of his shorts' pocket were spread out on the counter, and he found the thin leather band he used to tie back his hair. He got that taken care of, and then leaned in toward the mirror, angling his face to make sure he'd done a good job shaving.

Normally he went a few days without touching a razor, but he knew Lindsey had sensitive skin. He'd seen the small stubble burn he'd left on her breast earlier. It wouldn't happen again. The inside skin of her thighs would be sensitive, too.

He took a deep breath. Thinking about all the things he wanted to do to her sent a shaft of heat to his cock. He glanced down, not surprised that he was getting hard. He doubted his body had returned to normal since the second they'd lain down together on the beach last night. He was still damn impressed with his willpower. Didn't know how much longer it would last.

Gripping his cock, he gave it a few firm strokes. He groaned, closed his eyes, ordered himself to wait. On the other hand, nothing he could do for himself would feel close to the rush of burying himself inside Lindsey.

FRESHLY SHOWERED, her hair squeaky clean, every little kink blown out smooth and here she was headed confidently to the pool of all places. She really should have thought to tell Rick to meet her somewhere else.

Although meeting at the bar for example would likely mean running into Mia or Shelby. Their eyes were going to pop out of their heads when they saw Rick. He didn't fit Lindsey's normal type, and it would be kind of cool to shock Shelby, the most adventurous of them, but Lindsey didn't want them all to meet yet.

It wasn't until she'd returned to the room that she remembered their dinner tonight. An annual event when they celebrated their three birthdays together, they'd saved it for Hawaii this year. She hadn't told Rick yet, and she'd hate for Mia or Shelby to say something before she had the chance.

She'd worn her bikini under her thigh-length gauzy cover-up, though she had no intention of getting in the pool. It was close to three, the sun was weaker and she hoped to get about thirty minutes of sunbathing on each side. She left the elevator, stopped briefly to check her legs. To her delight the self-bronzing lotion looked as if it had worked a bit.

The pool area wasn't too crowded. A few kids paddled around in the water, and mostly couples sat on the deck or at the outdoor bar. It took her a few seconds to locate Rick. He'd claimed a pair of chaise lounges in a semi-shady alcove near one of the two big rock waterfalls. She had to smile. Leave it to him to find the most private spot available.

He signaled that he'd already picked up beach towels from the hotel attendant, and she skirted the shallow end of the enormous pool to join him. His hair was slicked back, he wore sunglasses, red swim trunks and, darn it, a brown shirt. As soon as she reached him, he stood, and she got the same silly flutter inside that seemed to kick in whenever he got close.

She also realized his hair wasn't slicked back, but rather tied into a short ponytail. Funny, she'd thought she hated ponytails on men.

"Hmm, you smell good…vanilla," he said near her ear, and kissed her as if he hadn't seen her just two hours ago.

She pulled away. "Down, boy. We've got kiddies watching us," she said, only half-teasing, the imprint of his lips making her want more.

"Lucky for you," he murmured, one side of his mouth inching up. "This spot okay?"

"Perfect." She moved the chaise so that only her legs would be exposed to the sun while her upper body and face would be in shade. She dropped her bag onto the deck, then sprawled out on the beach towel he'd spread on the chair for her.

Chuckling, Rick scooted his lounger closer.

"What?"

He trailed the back of his fingers up the outside of her thigh until they disappeared under the cover-up. "You gonna let me see that bikini you're wearing?"

The featherlike touch made her tingly. "Are you gonna let me see what's under that shirt?"

He let out a hearty laugh. "No problem, sweetheart." He grabbed the neckline, remembered at the last second to take off his sunglasses and then jerked the T-shirt over his head. "Your turn."

A four-letter word Lindsey had never said in her life, never even considered allowing to pass her lips, popped into her head. She tried not to stare. She tried to breathe.

The reaction her flushed body was having to his chest and flat, muscle-ridged stomach astounded her. These were six-pack abs. She totally got it now. Holy crap.

"Lindsey?"

She forced herself to take a breath. "Yeah."

"Hey."

She lifted her gaze. No, she hadn't done the lifting after all. She'd had help. His fingers were hooked under her chin, and he slowly forced her to meet his eyes.

"Take that off," he said, his hazel gaze dark and sexy, indicating the cover-up. "Now."

She didn't bother with the buttons. She yanked up the hem, pulled the gauzy fabric over her head. And forgot about the sunglasses sitting on top of her head. She sensed them flying through the air, and then heard them bounce on the stone deck.

With a rueful smile, Rick pushed off the chaise and retrieved them for her. "They look okay," he said, re-claiming his seat and examining the lenses. "Not even a scratch." He passed them to her, his gaze flickering to her breasts.

"Thanks." The turquoise-and-white bikini was a tad skimpier than she might have chosen had it not been on sale.

His gaze roamed her chest, thoroughly surveyed her belly and hips, drew down her legs and then returned to linger on the swell of her breasts before he slid his dark glasses back on.

She couldn't be annoyed. Not after the way she'd ogled him. She watched him toss his shirt over the back of his chair. And noticed a long brown leather strip fall onto the deck. She bent to pick it up. "Is this yours?"

He shook out his tousled hair, combed it back with his fingers and then used the strip to redo his ponytail.

With his arms raised, every muscle in his chest, shoulders, arms and belly clearly defined, her mouth went so dry she could barely swallow. She forced herself to lie back, keep her focus on the kids splashing around in the pool, until she saw him fiddle with the back of his lounger.

That's when she saw the tattoo. It was small, high on his upper arm, some kind of squiggly design. She squinted, but couldn't make it out. Rick hadn't seemed the type. "You have a tattoo."

"Yep." He glanced wryly at his arm. "The one on my back was on purpose."

She hadn't seen it. Not even when he picked up her sunglasses, so it couldn't be too big and awful. She was about to ask him about it when her phone rang. It was Shelby. Lindsey thought briefly about letting the call go to voice mail, or hold out for a text, but Rick knew she'd been waiting to talk to them about tonight and he was eyeing her with curiosity.

She answered, wishing it were Mia on the other end. Shelby would have a dozen questions, and she'd be merciless. Normally, it wasn't a problem. Lindsey had little to hide. But she wanted Rick to herself for as long as she could have him. Selfish, yes, but this was her magical week, and she gave herself permission to be as selfish as she wanted.

8

To Lindsey's relief, it was Mia on the other end of Shelby's phone. The birthday dinner wasn't mentioned, and Lindsey hoped they'd forgotten that tonight was the night. When Mia asked where she was, instead of lying, Lindsey told her she'd be up to the room shortly.

She dropped the phone into her bag, and saw that Rick was lying back with his face to the sun, his eyes closed. But it was impossible for him not to have heard her side of the conversation. She wondered if she'd disappointed him by not bringing up their trip to the North Shore.

"I have a confession to make," she said, and he brought his head up. "On my way down here I remembered that my friends and I had planned a dinner tonight."

"Ah. Good thing I have a room." He didn't seem mad, or even disappointed. Which scored him major points. A lot of guys she knew would be sulking.

"The reason I didn't bring it up to them is because I honestly hoped they'd forgotten all about it."

He smiled. "Not because of me..."

"Totally because of you." She laughed softly. "I'm going to see them for the rest of my life. I only get to be with you for a week." She sighed when he reached over and closed a hand over hers. "Anyway, the dinner isn't a big deal. Our birthdays are three months in a row, and we've always made it a point to do a joint celebration once a year since we were living in different cities."

"When's your birthday?"

"The end of February. It was three weeks ago."

"That's right. You'd just had a birthday when we met. We're close. Mine is the beginning of April."

"Are you an Aries or a Taurus?"

"Aries." He shrugged. "Whatever that means."

"I don't know much about it myself, except my friend Shelby is an Aries, too."

"Is that good or bad?" he asked, a teasing note in his voice.

"Well, Shelby is gorgeous, smart, charming, witty, always the life of the party. Oh, did I say gorgeous?"

"I think so." Rick leaned over, closing the short distance between their chairs.

He didn't have to touch her, show her what he was after. She leaned in for the kiss, and this time when he lingered, she didn't resist. In fact, she was sorely tempted to suggest they go to his room.

She felt the tip of his tongue at the corner of her mouth, and parted her lips in invitation. He didn't accept right away, but took his time molding his lips to hers, changing the slant of his mouth, using more pressure, then less. When he finally entered her mouth, he swept his tongue inside with a devastating thoroughness that left her hot and prickling with anticipation.

Then he drew away and smoothed back the fall of her hair, exposing her fevered cheeks. "Later," he whispered.

"After you see your friends, after dinner. Come to my room."

"Yes." She sighed. And caught a glimpse of Mia and Shelby on the other side of the pool.

Oh, crap. Had they seen her?

"How about a drink?" Rick squeezed her hand, and then let go to signal the waitress.

"Sure." She smiled, while furtively keeping track of Mia and Shelby as they signed out beach towels from the pool attendant.

"A cola?"

"Mai tai."

He chuckled. "Man, when the gloves come off—"

The waitress stopped, tray in hand, and crouched beside Rick to take his order.

Lindsey saw then that her friends had spotted her. It was Shelby, of course, who clarified that fact by comically ogling Rick and making oh-my-God faces. In spite of herself, Lindsey laughed.

The waitress had just walked away, and Rick turned to her. "What?"

"You're about to meet my friends. Prepare yourself."

He followed her gaze. "Am I gonna get the third degree, or what?"

"Possibly. Mia's the lawyer, but she won't do the grilling. Shelby's wearing the pink bikini and sarong. She's the one you have to watch out for." And looking sexy as usual, Lindsey thought grudgingly.

"This should be good." Rick touched her face. "You're already blushing."

Lindsey shook her head in resignation, then pushed

her sunglasses up, using them as a hair-band. She lifted her brows in warning as they approached.

Naturally Shelby ignored her. Why had Lindsey foolishly thought she'd do otherwise?

"So you're Rick," Shelby began, blatantly sizing him up, her gaze lingering on the arm tattoo. "Kept our Lindsey out late last night, didn't you?"

Rick politely removed his sunglasses. "Late?" he said, frowning thoughtfully, amusement glittering in his hazel eyes. "More like all night."

"I like you." Shelby grinned at Lindsey. "You can keep him."

"You're so kind," Lindsey said sarcastically, then gestured to Mia. "This is Mia, my more mature friend."

In the middle of the introductions, Rick got to his feet. "Here. Take this. I'll get a couple more chairs."

"We aren't staying," Mia said, and Lindsey quickly agreed.

Shelby laughed, and then her gaze went in the direction of the beach and she sobered, her brows puckering. With her eyes, she communicated something to Mia, and then said, "We'll see you later, Linds."

A couple more pleasantries were exchanged, and then they quickly moved toward the bar.

Lindsey turned her head, curious as to what Shelby had been looking at. Some kids were building a sand castle on the beach, a pair of teenagers were horsing around, but nothing out of the ordinary.

"See, that wasn't too painful."

Her gaze drew back to Rick, who'd sunk back down onto the chaise. "You weren't there when I told them I'd given you a fake name."

He smiled. "I vaguely remember them that night we met. They came to the party with you, right?"

"You vaguely remember Shelby? Seriously?"

He slid another look at her retreating form. "She's pretty. So is Mia. But you," he said, taking possession of her arm and kissing her hand, "are in a whole different league."

She smiled, leaned close and whispered, "You are so getting laid."

He barked out a surprised laugh. Then stared at her, clearly as startled as she was.

She had to have somehow channeled Shelby. That was not something Lindsey would say. Except that she had, and now she didn't know what to do with it.

Relieved, she spied the waitress headed toward them with her tray full.

"Our drinks," she warned, when she saw a wicked gleam enter his eye. "They're coming."

Rick grabbed his T-shirt and slid his feet into his leather flip-flops. "Screw the drinks," he said a moment before the waitress approached. He took the check from her and scribbled his name, a tip and room number across the bottom. "We can order room service."

Lindsey blinked, and managed a weak, "Right."

RICK LEFT THE BEER he'd ordered, but she pulled on her cover-up and took her mai tai with her. While he returned the towels to the attendant, she stood at the edge of the lobby, slowly sipping the drink, her nose wrinkling with each tiny swallow, watching him. Damned if he knew what to make of the woman.

Just when he thought he'd figured her out, she surprised him yet again. It was those big innocent eyes that totally messed him up. Made him feel like an ass when all he could think about was stripping her naked and laying her down on that king-size bed upstairs.

First, he knew better. She wasn't innocent. Second, he saw the way she'd looked at him earlier. She wanted it, too. If they'd been in his room instead of at the pool, he would've slid his hand between her thighs and found her good and wet.

It was official, she was killing him.

Walking toward her, he tossed his shirt over his shoulder. No use putting it on. They were going to his room, right now, and they *would* get naked. "You want your cherry?"

Her eyes widened. "What?"

He plucked the garnish off the side of her glass and held it up to her as they turned and walked toward the elevators.

"Oh, no. You can have the pineapple, too, if you want."

He popped the cherry into his mouth, and then helped himself to the pineapple wedge. "Don't worry, I'm not going to eat you, too." He smiled to himself. That was a lie. His good humor fled when he met those round startled blue eyes, saw the pink creep into her cheeks. "Stop blushing."

"I told you I can't help it," she said tightly, her wounded look shaming him.

"Hey, Lindsey, I'm sorry." He pulled her against his chest. "I am. I didn't mean it." He silently cursed himself, ignoring the people who had to step around them. "Go ahead and slap me if you want. I deserve it."

She flattened a hand on his chest. His heart pounded hard against her palm. "I wouldn't do that," she said softly. "But I do want to get out of everyone's way."

He dragged her to the side, where they were partially shielded by a tall potted palm. He gazed down at her upturned face. "I don't know why I said that. I actually like it when you blush. It's cute."

She frowned. "No, it's not. It's horrible, but out of my control. And if you hurt my feelings like that again, you'll have gotten that room upstairs for nothing." She blinked, and briefly glanced away. "At least as far as I'm concerned. Got it?"

"Got it," he murmured, struck by the quiet fierceness in her voice.

She took a deep breath. "Okay."

"Are we good?"

"We're good," she said, and took another sip of her drink.

"May I?" He lifted his brows to the drink. When she raised the glass to him, instead of taking it, he let her hold the mai tai while he took a pull. "Thanks." What he needed was a shot of tequila.

She surprised him yet again by pushing up on the tips of her toes and pressing a light kiss to his mouth. "I know I confuse you."

Rick couldn't help but laugh, though he withheld comment. He didn't want her to think he was looking for an excuse for his lousy behavior. The thing was, he was totally baffled by her. She was rockin' hot, and although she had been brought up by strict parents, she hung with hot, savvy friends who seemed far from shy. They'd gone to college together, shared apartments, now they were all going into business. Hard to believe she'd remained so sheltered. Yet he accepted it as the truth. Any effort at acting on her part had been spent on playing the worldly, experienced Jill. He'd seen through that facade quickly enough six years ago.

"We should go up," he said finally, and saw her visibly swallow at the same time she nodded. "We can order room service, and you can tell me about that new business of yours."

A slight frown tightened her brows, and for once he couldn't read her. He didn't like that much. "Shelby and Mia didn't say anything about the dinner, but I'd still like to check with them first, before we…"

"Absolutely," he said, holding up his hands. "You go do what you need to do. You have my number."

She smiled a little, as if she knew he wasn't above groveling at this point, then focused her preoccupied gaze on his arm.

Ah, the tattoo. She hadn't asked yet, but she would. And damn, but he'd have to explain.

LINDSEY ENTERED the elevator ahead of Rick, feeling the sting of disappointment when a couple rushed in behind him. His shirt was still draped over his shoulder, conveniently exposing the arm with the tattoo, and she jockeyed into a position that gave her a clear view. She was pretty sure she knew what it was now, and she very much wanted to ask him for confirmation, but not in front of anyone.

He looked up at the lighted floor panel at the same time she did. Seeing that they were coming up on her floor, he bent his head and kissed her. "I'll be waiting," he said, and kissed her again.

She nodded, avoiding eye contact with the other couple, and as soon as the doors slid open, scooted out of the car. It still boggled her mind that it had been only a day since they'd reunited. He was so easy with the touching and kissing, as if they'd been together for years. No one in her family had ever been demonstrative, including her. Sometimes she envied his ease, and sometimes she had to fight the instinct to pull away.

Since she'd seen Mia and Shelby only a little while ago, she didn't bother with a courtesy knock and let herself into the room. Once inside she felt a breeze, noticed that the balcony door was open and then saw Shelby sitting outside with a book on her lap. She looked up, and smiled. "Hey," she said, her gaze sweeping the room. "Are you alone?"

Lindsey nodded and dropped her purse on the closest bed. "I didn't expect to see you here."

"Ditto." The balcony was so small that there was room for only the one chair so Shelby came inside. "Oh, my God."

"What?"

"What?" Shelby mimicked in a mocking voice, and then with arched brows said, "Rick? Holy crap, you never said he was that smokin' hot."

Lindsey grinned. "The man does look good without a shirt. Where's Mia?"

"Forget Mia. Tell me everything."

No way that would happen. She knew Shelby often discussed her dates. Lindsey couldn't do it. Especially when the subject was Rick. And last night... She felt the heat in her cheeks thinking about how quickly he'd made her come, and she turned to look for a hair twisty that one of them normally left laying around. "We need to talk about our birthday dinner."

"You remembered? Are you insane? Why would you even come up for air?"

Laughing, she found a red twisty on the desk and pulled her hair back. "What are you doing in here reading?"

Shelby shrugged, climbed on the bed and sat cross-legged. "I have a date tonight, so I thought I'd come chill out before I have to get ready."

"Tonight? What about dinner?"

"Mia and I thought you'd forgotten. I know Mia had, although she wouldn't admit it. She's with David." Shelby paused, frowning. "You weren't here. You don't even know about David, do you?"

Confused, she shook her head and plopped down on the other bed. "I thought his name was Jeff."

"Oh, sweetie, you are so out of the loop. Jeff did show up, and he's a first-class ass. But that actually turned out to be a good thing. Remember her talking about her boss at the law firm? David Pearson?"

"*That* David? He's here?"

Shelby nodded, grinning. "He followed her here. Can you stand it?"

"Get out."

"You should see how he looks at her. It's almost disgusting," Shelby said cheerfully.

"Boy, I have missed a lot." Lindsey remembered Mia talking about David, especially in the beginning when she first started with the firm. But she'd given up hope long ago.

"Um…and what about you and Mr. Killer Body? Good God, is he one of those gym rats? He doesn't have that awful weight-lifter bulk."

"He surfs."

"Hmm…" Shelby thought for a moment. "I need to hit the beach more."

"You said you have a date tonight?" It took her a second to recall the guy's name from spring break. "With Josh?"

"Nope. Apparently he's married with a kid on the way." Shelby tossed her long tawny-colored hair, and with a sly smile added, "I met a lifeguard this morning, so it's all good."

"Of course you did." Lindsey wouldn't admit it but she was relieved. It would've been too hard to leave her friend alone tonight, though being dateless was seldom a problem for Shelby. "Where are you going?"

"Oh, no." Shelby wagged a finger. "You're trying to get out of telling me about Rick. Won't work. What's up with the tattoos?"

"To tell you the truth, I haven't seen the one on his back yet. But did you get a good look at his arm?"

"No." Shelby narrowed her puzzled gaze. "You haven't noticed his back?"

"I was otherwise occupied," she said crossly.

"Ah, right. I honestly didn't look closely enough, why?"

Lindsey hesitated. "I think it's a *J*."

"And?" Shelby drawled.

"Jill?" She waited for her friend's face to light with

comprehension. "He didn't have that tattoo the night we met."

Shelby let out a howl. "Did you ask him about it?"

"Not yet."

"You totally have to ask him."

"I will."

"I mean it, Linds. You have to. This is too funny."

"I know. I said I would," she said irritably, though *funny* isn't how she'd describe the situation.

Shelby regarded her speculatively. "You obviously made quite an impact on him."

"Don't get ahead of yourself. His mother's name could be Janet." She got to her feet. "What time is your date?"

"Soon." Shelby waved a hand. "Don't hang around because of me."

"Rick wants me to go to his place on the other side of the island. I'll be staying there a few days."

"He lives here?"

"Part-time. But look, I won't go if Mia is going to be tied up with David—"

Glaring, Shelby slid off the bed. "I'll help you pack."

9

LINDSEY PACKED ENOUGH things in her carry-on for three days. She couldn't imagine that she'd stay at Rick's longer than that. In fact, she wouldn't be surprised if he brought her back to Waikiki sooner. After getting over the initial shock of discovering his tattoo, she immediately started with the self-doubt, berating herself that she wasn't Jill, never would be, and that as soon as he figured that out, he wouldn't be interested. If he hadn't already decided he was wasting his time.

When she'd called him in his room he'd sounded as if he might have been dozing so she'd kept the conversation short, even offered to give him some space. He'd turned her down flat.

Only told her to hurry and get her sweet butt to the twelfth floor.

She found his room and knocked lightly in case he'd fallen asleep. He opened the door immediately. He still wore his swim trunks with no shirt, and she briefly wondered if she'd ever get tired of looking at his chest.

He smiled when he saw the bag and took it from her. "Come in," he said, stepping back.

She walked in, her gaze going straight to the glass doors and the view of the sparkling blue ocean beyond the large balcony. "Wow. Nice."

"I was lucky to get this at the last minute." He carried her bag through a doorway into another room.

She saw then that he had a suite. "Was this all they had left?" she asked, following him into the bedroom.

"No, but I wanted an ocean view." He set her bag on the dresser of highly polished mahogany, unlike the less expensive bamboo style used in her economy room.

"But it's such a waste."

He turned and frowned. "Are you kidding? Look at that." He gestured to the large plate glass window, framing the sunset and ocean as if they were a piece of art. "How can you call that a waste?"

"It's beautiful," she said, mesmerized by the water's varying hues of blue and green that could be seen from this height. "And that balcony you have out there is to die for." She jerked her head toward the parlor. "Ours is the size of a closet. But like I told you on the phone, we've postponed our dinner. I can go with you to your place."

"Good. We'll go later after we have a nap and some dinner." He grabbed her wrist and tugged her toward the bed. "Or tomorrow morning."

She felt bad. This unnecessary expense was mostly her fault. "But you didn't need a room. I don't have to be here tonight. Maybe you can still check out and pay for only half a day."

He smiled, sat at the edge of the bed and pulled her between his legs. "I'm not checking out. I'm keeping it as long as you're here."

"What? That's crazy."

"I like this dress." He put his arms around her waist and slowly rubbed her fanny. Eye level to her breasts, he pressed a kiss on the skin left exposed by her lime-green sundress.

"Rick, let's be sensible," she said, her logic and will-power already getting fuzzy as his lips trailed down the V. He used his teeth and tongue just the way she liked it, and slid his hands underneath the hem of her dress. "Rick…"

"Hmm?"

"You're not listening," she said, her breath catching when he molded his slightly rough palms over her butt. The silk panties might as well have not been there for as little protection as they provided from the seductive heat of his hands.

"Relax, Lindsey, it's only money," he said, working his fingers beneath the elastic. "But if you're having trouble chilling, you know I can help with that."

She saw the beginnings of a smug smile and shoved him hard enough to slam him back against the mattress. He only laughed, and took her with him. Then he groaned a little, and fearing she had hurt him, she pushed up, trying to take some of her weight off his body. Then she felt his arousal pressing her belly and she slumped back against him, her breasts crushed to his hard chest.

He tucked a tendril of hair behind her ear. "I have you right where I want you."

"I was thinking the same thing."

His brows shots up. "Wait. One minor adjustment."

He reached behind her neck and unknotted the halter part of her dress.

She held her breath, lifting slightly to allow him access while he pulled down the triangles of fabric and uncovered her bare breasts. Her nipples were taut and achy, and when they touched his naked chest she whimpered.

"Ah, Lindsey." His arms came around her and he hugged her so tightly she got a bit light-headed. "I can't seem to keep my hands off you."

"I noticed."

"Or my mouth." He nuzzled the side of her neck, then pressed light kisses across her collarbone.

She shuddered, and slowly, deliberately moved her hips against the hard hot bulge that seemed to have grown harder still.

He rolled over, pinning her to the mattress. Unprepared, she let out a startled squeal. Brushing his thumb across her lips, he said, "Keep that up and we'll find out if security remembers us from six years ago."

Lindsey chuckled. "Wouldn't that be funny?"

"Not so much."

"Thanks to you we made a clean getaway."

"I had ulterior motives." He bent his head and drew a nipple into his mouth, swirling his tongue over the sensitive flesh.

She gasped, and clutched his muscled shoulders, her entire body tingling with awareness. It didn't take much for him to get her revved up. It was almost embarrassing.

He lifted his head. "We're going to order some room service," he said, and laved her other nipple. "We'll eat on the balcony." He licked the skin between her breasts. "Share a nice bottle of wine."

The cool air danced across her damp nipples, making her shiver. Or maybe it was the way he stared at her, his eyes dark with promise and danger, as if his plans for her landed on the other side of wicked. The thought triggered a delicious tingle of anticipation.

"We'll feed each other dessert." He lightly scraped his teeth against her nipple, then soothed it with his tongue. "What's your favorite dessert, Lindsey?"

"Why?" she asked, trying to hide her smile.

"I'm hoping it involves a lot of whipped cream."

"And chocolate syrup?"

He peered at her with an amused lift of a brow. "Could get messy."

Not with your clever mouth.

The words were there in her head, on the tip of her tongue. Both Shelby and Mia would've shamelessly flirted with utter confidence. Why couldn't she be so bold just once? But she had when she told him he'd get laid. And then she'd stumbled, totally fallen on her face.

Rick kissed her chin, then flipped onto his side, held himself up by his elbow as he leaned over her. "What are you thinking, Lindsey?" he asked quietly, letting his hand rest on her belly.

She'd totally blasted the mood to smithereens. Feeling self-conscious, she pulled up the front of her sundress. His sudden mournful expression briefly eased the tension, and she managed a weak smile.

Anything she said at this point would be lame. "Tell me about the tattoo on your arm."

He sighed as if resigned. "It's a J," he admitted in a reluctant drawl.

She knew then she'd been right, and her pulse raced stupidly. Though getting a tattoo was big, permanent, not something you did on a whim. Well, she wouldn't. "Janet? Josephine? Janice? Come on, the suspense is killing me."

Disbelief flickered in his eyes, and then his gaze narrowed menacingly and he was all hands and mouth, tickling and nibbling at her until she pleaded and hiccupped for him to stop.

He gave her a minute to catch her breath, and it occurred to her that while she wasn't exactly Jill with him, she wasn't Lindsey, either. At least she was headed in the right direction.

The halter part of her dress had slipped down in the tussle, and his interest had returned to her nipples. She swatted him away as she covered herself. "No way. Tell me about the tattoo."

"I got it the day you left. I woke up. You were gone, and I had no clue how to find you."

"So you got a tattoo?"

He gave her a wry smile. "No, I got drunk first."

"That's crazy."

"Hindsight's a beautiful thing, huh?" He worked his hand underneath one of the rearranged triangles, and cupped her bare breast. He must have felt the quickening beat of her heart, and her nipples were still achingly hard. But he simply rested his hand there as if it were the most natural thing in the world.

"I was virtually a stranger," she said, trying to make sense of his behavior. "You didn't strike me as being that—" She stopped, appalled at what she'd been about to say.

"Foolish?"

"I only meant that you'd seemed more mature than the other guys," she said, her eyes closing as she leaned into his palm, aching for him to do something more. "How do you expect my brain and mouth to work in sync with you touching me like that?"

"Okay, I'll stop." Clearly trying to suppress a smile, he laid back and folded his hands on his belly. "Better?"

She tugged at her dress, making sure her breasts were covered. The friction of the sateen fabric rubbing her aroused nipples made her tremble. Hiding her reaction, she retied the halter at the back of her neck. "Much better," she agreed. "Thank you." She looked at him with every ounce of innocence she could muster.

It was totally worth it when his jaw dropped and he whined like a kid who'd dropped his ice cream cone.

Good. She'd surprised him. "Now," she said calmly, rolling onto her side and placing her hand on his chest. The tips of her middle and ring fingers grazed his flat brown nipple and he tensed. "What were you saying?"

"You expect me to be able to think when you're touching me like that?"

"Oh, I'm sorry," she said, coaxing the hard brown nub to life. "Want me to stop?"

"Hell, no." He moved his hands and clasped them behind his head, his mouth sporting a half grin.

This was her chance. She'd wanted to map his body with her hands, feel the hard muscle bunch beneath her palms. She really liked that his skin was so smooth and sleek. Only a small patch of hair arrowed down below his navel and disappeared underneath the waistband of his swim trunks.

Her gaze lingered there, her breath stuttering into short jerks when she saw that he was getting hard. She blinked and refocused her attention on his chest. His nipples weren't flat anymore. They were like small saucers holding tiny brown pearls.

She swallowed, and moistened her lips, the sudden realization that they had parted forcing her gaze back to his face. He was watching her with an intensity that made her want to look away, lie back, let him take the lead.

Instead, she moved her hand down his chest, over his belly and cupped the hardness straining his trunks. He hissed out a breath as she molded her palm to his arousal. Her hand shook slightly, but Rick didn't seem to mind.

He briefly closed his eyes, and then opened them to slits, his dilated pupils eclipsing the flecks of gold and green that had glinted with humor and lust only seconds ago. When he moved his hands from behind his head, she'd expected him to reach for her, but instead he fisted them at his sides. He clearly liked having her touch him, liked that she'd taken control.

To her amazement, she found that she liked it, too. The freedom to learn the contours of his body, to slide her hands anywhere she pleased, was almost dizzying. His skin was taut and as smooth as a marble sculpture. He had a couple of scars, a small one at the top of his rib cage, and a thin longer version at the side of his waist.

She came up on her knees beside him and traced the mark with her finger, then followed the muscular definition of his ridged belly. When she retraced the path with soft slow kisses, he moved his hips, just a bit, enough to let her know that he wanted her mouth lower.

Oh, God, she wasn't ready for that. Not yet.

Instead she stayed focused on his belly, kissing the warm smooth skin under his rib cage, then over his ribs and lingering on each nipple, using her tongue and teeth just as he had done to her.

Tension seemed to thrum through his body. He moaned. His chest heaved, then came down with a small shudder. Warmed by his response, she trembled a little, too, knowing she'd done that to him. Encouraged, she stroked his belly, then ran her palm over the long length of his hard penis. The barrier of the trunks frustrated her. She slipped her fingers underneath the waistband, brushing the silky smooth crown and then retreated.

Murmuring her name, Rick threaded a hand through her hair. He cupped her nape, forcing her to meet him halfway as he curled up to kiss her mouth, to push his tongue between her lips. His other hand covered hers, pressed it down, increasing the pressure of her palm on his erection.

Abruptly he released her hair, released her hand and caught her by the shoulders. In the next second, he had her on her back. He pulled down the top of her dress, greedily suckled one nipple and then the other. Her hair had fallen in a tangle over her shoulder, getting in the way. He gathered a handful, brought it to his face, inhaled deeply, then let the strands sift through his fingers. Gently he smoothed her hair aside, then kissed her exposed shoulder. He leaned back, and simply looked at her, her face, her throat, her breasts, his damp lips curving in a slow dangerous smile.

Their eyes met and she stared at him, unable to look away, even when he slid his hand under her dress, up the outside of her thigh. He could do anything to her, she realized, and she wouldn't stop him. The thought should've been enough to alarm her. She simply wasn't that comfortable with sex. She didn't like that she was inhibited, or that she couldn't be more casual about it, but wishing didn't chase the self-consciousness away.

"Take off your dress," he whispered.

She held her breath as he skimmed his palm over her hip, pausing at the narrow elasticized band of her silk panties. She exhaled when he withdrew his hand. "Will you take that off for me?" he asked again, and kissed the tops of her breasts.

She glanced at the window, at the open drapes. The golden glow of the late afternoon sun filled the room.

"No one can see inside, but I'll close the drapes if you want," he said, his voice a low seductive murmur near her ear.

What she wanted was for him to peel off her dress, and not have to strip while he watched. "Maybe just a little," she said, and sat up, intent on doing it herself.

He caught her hand. "You're nervous."

"No, I'm not," she denied a bit too hotly, and scooted off the bed so he wouldn't see her blush.

She pulled the drapes closed halfway, while trying to hold her dress up with her free hand. He was right. No one could see inside. But she wasn't keen on having so much light in the room. She turned and noticed that a shaft of sunlight fell across the bed, and she went back to fussing with the drapes until she got it just so.

When she looked at him again, she saw that he was trying to control a smile and she shrunk inside. How could a man like him be interested in her at all? She wanted to disappear. Grab her purse, run back to her room and shut out the world that she couldn't quite seem to fit in.

"Lindsey, hey." He was up and off the bed in seconds.

She blinked at him, not sure if she'd unwittingly said something horrible out loud.

He put his arms around her and hugged her against his chest. "How about we look at the room service menu?"

His arousal prodded her belly, but that was changing. He wasn't so hard anymore.

"Why? I thought we were..." She moistened her lips. "Going in another direction."

"I want to make love to you, Lindsey." He drew back to look at her. "I couldn't lie about that if I wanted to."

"But you've lost interest," she said, miserable, and unable to meet his eyes.

He nudged her chin up. "You think I don't want you? Seriously?"

Anything she could think to say would make her sound like she was twelve. Heck, she'd read online how even twelve-year-olds were sexting. Great. That made her the emotional equivalent of ten. She gave a dismissive shrug. "If you'd rather eat, that's okay. Call room service."

Rick sighed. "I want to make love to you. But not until you're ready."

"Ready? It isn't as if this is our first time." She sounded properly indignant for someone who was about to shrivel up and die of humiliation.

He studied her for a moment. "You're right," he said, a thin smile curving his mouth. "I'm punchy. Not enough sleep."

"We could take a nap before dinner."

"Yeah, we could." He leisurely rubbed her arm, then brought her hand up for a quick kiss. "Sound good to you?"

She nodded, feeling silly for reacting to the casual touch. The thing was, she really did want him to make love to her. She was still hypersensitive, aching for the feel of his hands and mouth. She simply wasn't sure about taking the lead. Which was horrifically pitiful. He'd only wanted her to pull off her dress, not do a striptease. Maybe.

"You turn down the bed," he said. "I'll close the drapes the rest of the way."

"Not on my account," she said quickly.

"I can't sleep with this much light."

She neatly folded the thick floral coverlet to the foot of the bed, suspicious that he was darkening the room because he'd sensed her edginess. The skittish behavior had to stop. She waited until he ducked into the bathroom, then quickly pulled off her dress and slipped between the sheets.

10

RICK SPLASHED HIS FACE with cold water, dried off and stared at his reflection in the mirror. His hair had gotten wet and he slicked it back. He checked his chin and jaw. Still smooth from his recent shave. Probably should've gotten a haircut last week though. He never thought of those kind of things until it was really bugging him, or he was about to get on a plane to visit the folks. His mother and sister always nagged him about his long hair.

Once he'd made the mistake of wearing a ponytail to the house. His brothers hadn't stopped giving him crap about that for a week, and their good-natured arm-wrestling contests had ended with four broken fingers and a shattered lamp that had belonged to his grandmother. He did feel bad about the old lamp. Both his brothers deserved wearing splints for three weeks.

He straightened, glanced down at his trunks and rubbed his cock. One more ignored hard-on and he was likely to bust something else. He had to start using his head. Lindsey was fine as long as he kept the ball rolling between them. She wasn't good at initiating or being thrust in the spotlight. He was still learning her, and she was certainly different. The only woman he'd been with in a long time that he actually could take home to meet the folks.

The rogue thought stopped him.

He wasn't ready to do anything like that. Hell, he never considered getting serious with anyone. He still had too much to do. Like figure out how he could shave an ounce off the next generation surfboard. They'd gotten lighter, smaller, more adept. Wally thought he was crazy, and maybe Rick had gotten too ambitious, possibly even too desperate....

Yeah, he was crazy. A smart guy would sit back and enjoy life. It wasn't as if he had to worry about ending up in a four-wall box for eight hours every day and answering to a boss if he didn't come up with a new mind-blowing discovery.

He shook his head at his reflection. No more thinking. Lindsey couldn't have come at a more perfect time. This week was about reconnecting, having fun, having sex. Hopefully.

He hung the towel on the rack, used some mouthwash, then left the bathroom, hoping she'd still be there. Though not dark, the room was dim, and it took a second for his eyes to adjust.

She was already tucked in, lying on her side, the sheet and blanket pulled up to her chin. He smiled as he rounded the bed, surprised when out of the corner of his eye he saw her dress draped over the arm of the chair. His heart slammed his chest.

He hesitated, staring at the back of her head, the mass of silky blond hair, trying to decide if he should take off his trunks. Damn, he wanted to slide his naked body between the sheets and press his cock against that firm sweet ass. Wanted her long shapely legs wrapped around his hips. He wanted to watch those big blue eyes lose the panic and fill with satisfaction when he slid inside of her and made her come.

His thumbs were already hooked in his waistband. He inhaled deeply, waited for his head to clear. Leaving on his trunks, he got under the covers, watching her, waiting for her to acknowledge him. She stirred slightly, but kept her face averted. He moved closer, sliding an arm around her waist, and smiled a little because she still wore her panties. He tightened his arm and hauled her body against his, pleased that she hadn't tensed.

"Are you awake?" he whispered, and kissed the back of her shoulder.

"Yes."

"Should I set an alarm?" He stroked her belly, and then cupped her breast. Her nipple was firm and tight.

"I don't see why."

He buried his face in the side of her neck, letting the scent of her sweet skin fill his nostrils. Naturally he was hard again. Not a damn thing he could do about it. He would wait for her to make the first move. "Go to sleep," he murmured, his fingers flexing, unconsciously kneading her breast.

She made a soft sound, a quiet moan of pleasure that sent a shaft of heat straight to his cock. He closed his eyes, gritted his teeth. If she turned around, if she tried to touch him, that was it. He'd coax those panties off her. Find out if she was as tight a fit as he remembered.

She moved, as if trying to get comfortable, and

snuggled her ass more firmly against his cock. She stilled suddenly, no doubt having discovered how hard he was.

Screw it. He was taking off his trunks. He started to roll over, when she shifted, moved away and then turned over to face him. She closed in, and pressed her breasts against his chest.

They both shuddered.

She gave him a hesitant smile. "Can we sleep like this?"

Not trusting his voice, he could only nod, and dropped an arm around her.

LINDSEY AWOKE, surprised that she'd actually fallen asleep. The room was darker now but she didn't need to see to know that Rick was there with her. Half her body was draped over him. Her naked body. His naked body. No, he still had on swim trunks. She still wore panties.

She gathered her hair at the back of her neck, afraid the ends would tickle him awake as she stretched up to see the bedside clock. It was nine-thirty. Wow, she really had slept. Had he been asleep the whole time, she wondered, as she settled back down. Her nipple grazed his hard chest, and her entire body reacted with a shiver of pure longing.

His head jerked, and she thought she'd woken him. But he didn't open his eyes, only scraped his jaw against the pillow, so maybe inadvertently she had tickled him. He still had one arm around her, or rather she had it pinned to the mattress with her body. She didn't dare move to free him. She wanted to simply stare at him without being self-conscious about it.

A faint stubble of beard had begun to shadow his jaw and made the dimple in his chin look deeper. His hair had fallen back and she thought she saw a tiny hole in his earlobe. She hadn't noticed him wearing an earring. Peering closer she discovered that it was a tiny freckle.

She liked his hair. It was darker than it looked under the interesting blend of sun-streaked highlights. She counted three shades of gold and mused how unfair it was that women had to pay so much money for the same effect. But of everything she admired about his face, she liked his mouth the best. It was wide, his lower lip slightly fuller than his top one, and his smile…oh, his smile actually had the power to make her weak in the knees.

"Are you hungry?"

At the unexpected sound of his voice, she jumped. His eyes were still closed, but those lips she'd been staring at lifted in a small smile that said he knew he'd startled the heck out of her.

"How long have you been awake?" she asked accusingly.

He opened one eye and squinted at her. "Long enough," he said, and tried to curl his arm around her waist. "Ouch. My arm's still asleep."

She snorted. "You get no sympathy from me."

Rick eyed her with amusement as he flexed his arm, made a fist with his hand and then relaxed it. "Wait 'til I get some blood circulating. We'll see who needs sympathy."

Her stomach chose that second to rumble noisily.

She blushed, then grinned at his comical expression.

"Sorry, I didn't get that," he said, lifted the covers and pressed an ear to her belly.

She gasped, laughed, shoved at his shoulder. "Stop it."

"Shh, we're trying to have a conversation down here."

"Rick," she drawled out in a warning when he slid lower.

He turned his head and kissed her belly. Then kissed her through her panties. When he got to the juncture of her thighs, she stiffened, but didn't stop him. Only watched, waited, her heart pounding so hard she feared her body might come off the mattress.

He lifted his head, trailed the tip of his finger along the elastic around her leg, then slowly slipped it underneath. Instinctively she squeezed her thighs together. He hesitated, only for a second, and as his gaze found hers, he gently nudged her legs apart and slid his long finger between the folds of her sex.

Closing her eyes, she let her head fall back, forced herself to breathe evenly, ordered herself to relax. She was nervous. Not because of what he was doing but because of the proximity of his mouth. She knew she wasn't ready for that, and if he headed in that direction, well she simply didn't know what...

He touched her clit and she bit off a gasp, clutching at the sheets.

Shuddering, she stared at him, unable to make out his expression in the dimness of the room.

He moved up so that his mouth hovered over hers. His

hand stayed cupped over the damp crotch of her panties. "What do you want, Lindsey?" He slowly rubbed his palm over her panties, over her clit. "Tell me."

Overwhelming need swept through her body. Desperate for his touch, she shivered. "I want you to make love to me."

His mouth, already open, came down over hers, his tongue urgently seeking her participation. She put her arms around his neck, then held very still when he shoved her panties down past her hips. He broke the kiss, took her arms from around his neck and laid them at her side. He slid down to kiss each breast, swirled his tongue around her navel and then pulled her panties all the way off.

Lindsey watched him as he leaned back and looked at her. Just looked.

"You, too," Lindsey said softly, subtly pressing her thighs closer together.

He dragged his gaze away, and then slid up the front of his body, his chest skimming her belly, her breasts, and then he kissed her lips. "What, sweetheart?"

She cleared her throat. "Your trunks."

He smiled. "Sure." He was off the bed in a flash, his trunks sailing toward the chair near the window, clearly not a self-conscious bone in his body. "How about a little light?"

She didn't answer, but stared after him as he walked to the bathroom, fully erect. She wanted to touch him. Very badly. The idea shocked her. She never had those urges, at least not to the extent that she ached with the wanting now.

A light came on in the bathroom, though not the

overhead one. Maybe it was the small recessed light over the tub because by the time the illumination reached the room, it was a soft sensual glow.

Rick reappeared, and she saw that he had a condom packet in his hand. "This light okay?"

"Yes." God, she hated that her voice sounded so tight. Hated that he was backlit, and she couldn't see him well enough.

"Or we could turn on the lamp."

"No."

"All right." He dropped the packet on the nightstand and climbed into bed, stretching out beside her.

To Lindsey's dismay, she faced the light, which was to his back. She really wanted to see more of him, even while she understood exactly how totally hypocritical that was on her part.

Rick gently smoothed back her hair, rearranging it over her shoulder and exposing her right breast. When he ran the pad of his thumb across her nipple, she arched her back, and his mouth came down fast, his tongue darting out to flick the pearled tip.

Slowly she reached between them and found his hard penis. He jerked at the touch, but stilled as she curled her hand around the thick hot shaft and stroked the length of him. She stopped at the crown, using her thumb to learn the silky smooth softness already beading with moisture. It didn't seem possible that any part of him could be this soft, and to her complete amazement, she had the sudden urge to know the feel of it against her lips.

She wouldn't be so bold, of course. Mostly she was

afraid she'd do it wrong. No, the truth was, she was simply afraid of that kind of intimacy.

"Here." Rick molded his hand over hers, forcing her to grip him tighter, and then guided her hand down his penis, back up again, showing her how much pressure to use.

A low moan of pleasure tore from his throat. He squeezed her hand, quickened the rhythm before releasing her.

As fascinated as she was that he seemed to grow impossibly harder beneath her palm, she was mortified that she had to be shown what to do. But she didn't let up, not until he stilled her hand.

"You show me now," he said, pressing his palm against hers, and then curling his fingers over her hand.

She stared blankly at him.

"Show me what you like." He brought her hand to her pubic area. "Show me, Lindsey."

She jerked it back. "I like what you do to me," she said, hoping he'd leave it at that.

"Okay." He nodded. "Okay." He moved over her, his arousal laying hot and hard and heavy across her belly, and she held her breath, waiting to see what he was up to.

He plucked the packet off the nightstand, and then leaned back, turning some, so that the light now shone a bit on him. Her gaze went to his penis, the crown slick with moisture. Even with her sadly limited experience with the male anatomy, she knew he was big, and if they hadn't already done it, she might have worried about the fit. But she remembered very well how he'd squeezed inside of her, how he'd pushed deeper and deeper, filling

her until she thought she was going to die from the pleasure of it.

"Touch me if you want," he said, and her gaze flew up
to his. He was studying her face, his knowing expression
nearly her undoing. "Anywhere, anyway you want."

How naive she must seem to him. She shrank back,
wondering what the heck had happened to her grand plan
to become the irrepressible Jill. She wished he'd climb
on top of her and get on with it already. She wanted him.
She'd asked him to make love to her.

He touched himself, stroking his penis a couple of
times, fascinating her with the ease with which he regarded his sexuality.

She ignored the urge to hide her face in the pillow,
took a deep breath and came up on one elbow. With her
free hand, she learned the underside of his penis, then
cupped his balls.

He sucked air in between his teeth.

She froze, widening her eyes as she stared up at
him.

Briefly he closed his eyes, and then stroked her cheek-
bone with the pad of his thumb. "You look as if I'm
forcing you to do something you don't want to do."

"That's not true," she said quickly. "It's not. Please."
She lifted herself higher, pressed a quick kiss to his
firm mouth.

Indecision flickered across his face. His lips thinned.
"Take the condom."

She did, fumbling with the packet and finally tearing
it open.

"You do it," he said when she tried to pass it to him.
She got up on her knees and carefully rolled the

condom down his engorged penis. Her hands shook slightly, and he pressed them between his warm palms, brought them to his lips.

He kissed her fingertips before releasing her and taking her by the shoulders. "Lie down," he said, and guided her with a gentle force that somehow excited her.

In seconds she was on her back, and he was kissing her, leisurely, thoroughly, and she opened her mouth and her thighs to him.

When he drew back, his hair had fallen across his forehead, and she pushed it aside so she could look at him. He smiled down at her, his eyes almost the color of warm honey. He splayed a hand between her breasts as he moved into position between her legs.

Her lids fluttered closed, but when he entered her so quickly, she jerked, eyes wide, then realized he'd used only his fingers.

The devastation in his face stopped her.

"Rick?"

He shook his head, leaned back. "You're wet," he murmured, glancing at his slick fingers. "But I'm scaring you."

"No." She caught his arm, pulled at him. "I want you inside me," she whispered in a broken voice. "Please." She spread her legs wider apart, lifted her hips.

His hooded gaze drew to her eyes, and his tongue dampened his lower lip.

"Now, Rick."

He grabbed hold of himself and rubbed her with the tip of his sheathed penis. The friction made her whimper, made her buck toward him. He began to move, pushing into her, slowly at first and then driving in deep until a strangled cry tore from way down in her throat.

Lindsey pressed the back of her hand to her mouth, afraid she'd make too much noise. He shoved her hand aside and kissed her hard, his tongue making a thorough sweep of her mouth. When he finally leaned back, he cupped her hips and pulled her up to meet his thrusts.

He muttered an apology, an oath, another apology as he threw his head back, his jaw clenching. The realization hit her that he was struggling for control and excitement surged from her belly into her chest. She wrapped her legs around his hips and moved against him, matching his rhythm, taking him in deeper and deeper. The way he moved, his penis rubbed against her with each thrust, not just inside, but against her clit, and she didn't remember that from before. She hadn't known it was even possible.

She felt her body tense as he moved faster, right there, and just when she thought she couldn't take any more, the spasms racked her body. She came as she'd never come before. She cried out, gripped him so hard she could feel his muscles tremble. She barely noticed when he collapsed on top of her.

11

Lying on his side, Rick watched Lindsey sleep, her pink lips slightly parted, her hair a cloud of gold spread over the pillow. The early morning sun streamed in through a narrow gap where the drapes barely came together and a shaft of sunlight fell across her bare shoulders. Her skin was so damn smooth, so soft, flawless. She was like that all over. Didn't seem possible, but he was pretty sure he hadn't missed a spot.

He smiled and yawned, wanting very badly to touch her, but he wouldn't risk waking her. It wouldn't be fair after keeping her up most of the night.

After she'd loosened up, she'd surprised him with her eagerness to learn. He'd never played the teacher role before and he actually enjoyed the experience. Even when he'd popped his cherry at fifteen it had been with an older college woman. Of course there hadn't been any instruction going on. The whole thing had happened embarrassingly fast.

Lindsey stirred, but she was still asleep. Slowly he peeled back the sheet and examined the red mark on her neck. It bothered him to know he'd done that to her.

Unintentionally, but it didn't matter. It was there with no way of erasing it.

Thinking he saw her eyelid twitch, he stayed perfectly still, watching, waiting, hoping she'd get more sleep, hoping she'd wake up and kiss him.

She was amazing. It wasn't just her looks, although she rocked that department, too. She was brave and much stronger than she seemed to think. It was always easier to follow the crowd, do something because everyone else did it. Lindsey held her ground on certain principles, and she sure as hell wasn't a pushover.

He saw her lid twitch again, then she wrinkled her nose. Making a small fist, she stretched one arm above her head, arched her back and slowly opened her eyes. They widened on him as if she'd forgotten he was there. Then she blinked, tucked in her hand, her lips curving in that shy smile he liked too damn much.

"Hey," he said, gently kissing her cheek.

She primly pulled the sheet up to her throat. "What time is it?"

He hid a smile and tugged at the sheet. "Hmm, you have something down there I haven't seen yet?"

She gave him a dirty look. "You're hilarious."

"Come on. Let me see if I missed anything." He ducked his head under the covers.

Laughing, she pulled his hair.

"Ouch." He shot back up. "I guess I need a haircut."

Lindsey frowned. "I usually like short hair on men, but I don't know, I kind of like it long," she said, moving a shoulder. "It suits you."

"What? The beach-bum look?"

"Is that what you are?" The teasing glint in her eye

was gone with a blink, and for a few awkward seconds neither of them spoke.

She didn't have to say it. She wouldn't be happy with a man who had no ambition or goal in life. She was too smart, too sensible. She believed in long-term plans.

He had the sudden urge to tell her about the patent, how he never had to work another day if that's what he chose. She'd be more impressed with his current project, not the product itself...she wouldn't give a crap about a lighter surfboard, but that he was actively working and so close...

But close didn't cut it. He'd been "close" for two years now. Just as he'd been close to designing the next generation camber profile snow ski, until someone else had beat him to it.

Nah, there was nothing to tell her. He'd end up opening the door to questions he didn't want to think about, much less answer. Almost thirty and he'd accomplished nothing in the past ten years. Pretty sad that he'd done all his best stuff by twenty.

"Hey." He placed a hand on her belly, then briefly cupped the small patch of trimmed blond hair below, the one place his mouth hadn't been. She'd told him she wasn't ready, and he hadn't pushed it.

She squirmed, smiled a little. "'Hey' what?"

"It's seven-thirty. I'm starving. We can either order room service, or get on the road and stop somewhere along the way."

"Room service. I need—" She jerked, breathed a soft gasp when he slid a finger against her. "Coffee."

Dammit, he was hard. He flipped the sheet back, and her gaze went straight to his cock. He pumped it once, a second time. She didn't look away. Major progress. "I'll order," he said. "What else besides coffee?"

She threw off her side of the sheet and moved against his palm. "I bet we used up all the condoms."

"Nope. Only five."

"Only," she repeated with a mocking smile, then tensed, briefly closed her eyes, gasped again.

He touched her tightened right nipple. "Pancakes? Waffles? An omelet?"

She caught her lower lip with her teeth, slightly arched her back. "Surprise me."

"I intend to." Damn, they had used up the condoms that were on the nightstand. The box was in the bathroom. "Here." He took her hand, and cupped her palm over her pussy. "Keep this warm for me."

The color rushed to her cheeks and her hand stiffened. Obviously she wasn't crazy about that idea. The night had been one long exploration, sometimes they'd moved too fast and strained her comfort level. He'd made sure she knew none of it was a problem. If she'd pulled the sheet back over her body before he returned, he wouldn't be surprised.

He lightly kissed her lips, rolled his tongue over the nipple he'd abandoned. "Be right back."

"Rick?"

Since he'd already hit the floor, he stopped by her side of the bed.

She gingerly stroked his cock, looked up at him with those big blue eyes and said, "First the condom, then room service."

THE NORTH SHORE was a totally different world. Not just different from Waikiki, but different from anything

Lindsey had ever seen. Rick had described the area while he drove, but words couldn't capture the beauty of the lush green landscape and miles of breathtaking beaches.

Even the store where they'd stopped to pick up a bag of Kona coffee was quaint and full of characters. Both employees and three out of the four customers knew Rick, and it was interesting to watch and listen to him interact with them. He used a couple of phrases she didn't understand although she knew they weren't precisely Hawaiian words, she didn't think, but more likely local jargon.

While he paid the cashier, Lindsey waited outside the door of the small store, enjoying the ocean breeze coming from across the highway, and watching a heavyset older woman with long black hair liberally streaked with gray. She sat on the grass under a coconut tree, strumming a ukulele and singing to herself. Her woven hat and faded Hawaiian shirt had seen better days and her feet were bare, but she seemed at peace with her music, stopping only to scatter scraps of bread to the squawking birds.

"Last chance," Rick said as he joined Lindsey outside. "Need anything before we head to my place?"

Shaking her head, she frowned at the bag, suspicious of the brown box she'd glimpsed. "I thought you needed coffee."

A sly smile tugged at his mouth, and he opened the bag to her inspection. It was a box of milk chocolate macadamia nut clusters. Not one of the small boxes, either.

"You rat. You know I can't resist those darn things."

"Don't worry." He put an arm around her, kissed her hair and murmured, "I plan on working every calorie off you."

She smiled, having become more accustomed to his teasing. They walked toward the Jeep, and the woman in the hat looked up, her brown face lighting up with a big grin when she spotted Rick. She stopped strumming long enough to wave a thick hand, then went back to her music.

"Hi, Auntie Leialoha." Rick jerked his head toward the store. "Jimmy has two more loaves of bread for your birds."

"Mahalo, Rick." Still grinning, the woman gave him a reproving shake of her head. "God bless you."

"She lost her son in the Gulf War," Rick said softly. "She hasn't been the same since."

"You're related?" Lindsey asked when they got to the Jeep.

"Related? No." He paused. "Ah, she's not really my aunt. Around here it's a term of respect when you address someone older. Everyone calls her Auntie Leialoha. If I introduce you to some of the little kids they'll call you Auntie Lindsey."

"Really?"

"It's kind of weird at first, but you get used to it." His phone rang, and he dug it out of his pocket and checked the caller ID. "Sorry. I gotta take this."

"Go ahead." She climbed into the passenger seat and watched him round the front. Heard him address the caller. Apparently it was Wally, someone he'd spoken to earlier as they'd left the hotel.

He stopped, stared at the Hawaiian shaved-ice stand

across the street, and scowled over something he'd been told. He seemed really ticked off, and Lindsey tried not to eavesdrop, but this demeanor was such a contrast to Rick's easygoing manner that she couldn't help herself.

He slanted her a glance. Abruptly he turned away, raked a hand through his hair and dropped his voice to a low angry murmur.

A strong breeze swept off the water, picked up his voice and carried it to Lindsey just as he said, "I don't care what she says. Just make sure she's out of my house before we get there."

Lindsey stiffened. He was talking about another woman. Who was at his place? Or maybe Lindsey had heard wrong. His voice had been muffled, the wind sometimes distorted sound…

Come on, Lindsey. She had no right to be upset if he was involved with someone else. Of course he hadn't said anything about it, but if he were that callous…

Feeling a bit queasy, she pressed a hand to her stomach.

He swung in behind the wheel. "Sorry about that. Small change in plans. We're… Are you all right?"

"Fine." She pretended to smooth the front of her tank top, wishing her stomach would settle down. "A change in plans?"

"We're not going to my house yet. We're stopping at the shop."

"Your shop?" she asked, and he nodded. "I thought we were close to your place."

"We are."

"Maybe I could drop off my bag first." She kept her

gaze level with his, waiting for guilt to creep across his face.

"Give me a half hour." He didn't even blink. "In Motion is on the way."

"Sure." She turned her head and stared toward the vast blue ocean, aware that he was dividing his attention between her and reversing the Jeep.

He had to know something was wrong. Maybe he knew her better than she apparently knew him. If he was seeing someone seriously, then good for him. But he'd had no business showing up at the hotel to meet her.

Lindsey sniffed quietly. Or making her fall just a little bit in love with him.

"WHERE IS EVERYBODY?" Rick scooped a discarded gum wrapper off the tile floor and dropped it in a wastebasket behind the counter.

He'd taken her hand and led her into the large airy shop filled with surfboards. But it hadn't escaped her notice that he let go as soon as he saw the older man hefting a red-and-white board up onto a display shelf. He wore a tan tank top that showed off surprisingly buff arms and long baggy blue shorts the same shade as his rubber flip-flops. With his long wiry hair and unkempt mostly gray beard he looked like an aging hippie.

"Sunset," he said gruffly, turning to Rick. "Where do you think?" The man's piercing black gaze shifted to Lindsey. "You must be—" His bushy brows drew into a frown.

"Lindsey," Rick offered. "This old grouch is Wally."

"I'd shake your hand but I got crap all over mine." He inspected his rough callused palms, and muttered,

"No wonder since I've been doing all the work around here lately."

With a faint smile, Rick winked at her. "Wally runs the show and keeps everyone in line."

"Including you." Wally stared blatantly at Lindsey, his craggy face a perpetual frown, and then switched his attention to Rick. "She's a knockout. What's she doing with you?"

"Haven't figured that out yet." Rick hugged her against his side and kissed her heated cheek. "What did Deanna say? Does she want cash or credit applied toward her next board?"

"Cash," Wally said, glancing again at Lindsey, his speculative gaze moving over her face, down her body. Not insolent, but curious. "She just called. She split but didn't get to the patio."

Rick spread his hands. "The patio?" he said irritably. "What could they have—" He sighed, shook his head in defeat.

"Hey, bro, don't shoot the messenger." Wally chuckled, oblivious to Rick's annoyance. "You got a minute to go over some invoices?"

"No." Rick dug into his pocket, pulled out some cash and counted out a few twenties. "Is this enough?"

Wally shrugged. "Too much, but I know you'll give it to her anyway."

Lindsey walked over to a rack of T-shirts and tank tops, absently sifting through them as she vaguely listened to the men go back and forth. Rick sent her a couple of apologetic glances but she waved them off. The truth was, she was glad for the opportunity to be with her own thoughts. Her very morose thoughts.

She couldn't help but think this stop was a stall tactic. It made her sick to consider that Wally knew what Rick was doing. That he was buying time to get rid of one woman so he could replace her with another. Maybe that's why Wally had sized her up.

Clenching her teeth, she ordered herself to stop torturing herself. Rick was a free agent. So was she. Sure, last night had been incredible for her, more than she'd anticipated. It was supposed to be about sex, that's all, but she'd felt as if they'd connected on a different level, as if there might be a tiny spark that would carry them beyond this week. But apparently she was wrong. It wasn't his problem, it was hers. They had a silent agreement. One splendid hedonistic week of madness, and then back to their old lives. She couldn't blame him for actually having a life.

But deep down she did. She blamed herself, too, for thinking she was open-minded and sophisticated enough to walk away from the encounter unscathed. Good grief, what had happened to her? She was more sensible than this. She knew herself better than to risk becoming emotionally involved.

She breathed in, slowly breathed out, trying to clear her head. Maybe she was simply over tired and overreacting. Maybe there was another explanation for what she'd overhead. That was entirely possible.

Wally's hearty laugh pierced her preoccupation. He and Rick were trading barbs, which she doubted was for her entertainment. The two men seemed to have a gruff affection for one another and only an hour ago she would've enjoyed listening to them. Right now, all she wanted to do was to return to Waikiki. In fact, the next flight to Chicago wasn't out of the question.

"Hey." Rick was suddenly beside her, his hand at the small of her back. When he tried to kiss the side of her neck, she moved her head.

"The T-shirt you wore the other day," she said, avoiding his eyes. "It had your shop's logo. I didn't know—"

"Lindsey." He rubbed her back. "What's wrong?"

"Nothing." She darted a look toward the register where she'd last seen Wally. He wasn't there. "Your friend…he seems like a real character."

"Yep. I've known him for five years. He runs the shop. Whether I'm here or not. I don't know what I'd do without him."

"I'm glad for you."

He hesitated, and she knew he was studying her, trying to figure out what was going on, but she couldn't look at him. He read her too well, and she was feeling pretty miserable. And the last thing she wanted was his pity.

"Look," he said finally, "I only wanted to drop off the money and introduce you to Wally. We can leave anytime you want."

A nasty remark about the coast being clear teetered at the tip of her tongue, but she thought better of it. "Sure."

"Why don't you pick out some tanks and shirts for yourself and your friends? You know, a souvenir from the North Shore."

She looked at him then because he sounded nervous. His hazel eyes were dark and troubled as they met hers. Did he finally understand that she knew what was going on?

Silently, she cleared her throat. "We should go."

"Right. We'll be dropping by here again. You'll have more time to check out the merchandise." His mouth lifted in a worried smile. "Wally's in the back. I'll tell him we're leaving."

She managed to return his smile, desperately wanting to ask him about the phone call. She didn't want to say she'd eavesdropped, but more than that, she didn't want to see him lie. But this wasn't the time or place. She would ask him, though, either in the car or at his home. She'd be able to tell if he was hiding something, if there was someone important in his life. If necessary, she'd ask him to take her back to Waikiki, or she'd spring for a cab.

Heck, maybe she should just go ahead and do that anyway. No matter what, she already was in over her head.

12

HIS HOUSE WASN'T PRECISELY on the beach but sat on a large plot of partially wooded land across the two-lane road. He drove them down a short driveway and pulled the Jeep under a carport attached to a single-story wood house.

The coastal drive had been short, under ten minutes, and with Rick enthusiastically pointing out the sights along the way, Lindsey still hadn't decided how to broach the subject of her return to Waikiki. Every time she snuck a glance at him, or he flashed that darn big Hollywood smile at her, her resolve weakened. Hadn't he given her exactly what she'd come for? Fun and sex.

She cringed just thinking of how slutty that sounded, and then gave herself a mental shake. Sex was a natural healthy impulse. Though they didn't sleep around, Mia and Shelby were sexually active. No one judged them, and no one should. It was time to cut herself some slack.

She had only four full days left in Hawaii. There was no reason she couldn't ignore that stupid brain of hers and simply enjoy herself.

But then she flashed back on the stunning women she'd seen strolling the North Shore beaches, not tourists, but local women with hard tan bodies that could make a grown man weep, and her incredibly foolish brain went to that dark, dark place. North Shore seemed to be a small community. How many of them were sleeping with Rick?

She'd bet none of them would refuse Rick a darn thing. Or blush over his sexy suggestions. Why would he chase anyone out of his house for her? Was she simply a novelty? Flavor of the week? Her heart sank like an anchor to the pit of her stomach. Darn him for having made her feel so special, for making her romanticize that she was the only one in his life. Even if it was for one measly week. He was with her, not any of them, she reasoned. Couldn't she just enjoy the fantasy?

So much for turning off her doubts.

Caught up in her one-woman pity party, she hadn't realized he'd cut the engine and was staring at her. He reached for her hand, gave her a sad resigned smile. "What's wrong, Linds? You're not yourself." When she was too busy kicking herself to answer, he said, "You expected a nicer house, maybe?"

She hoped her glare told him what she thought of that remark. Then she just sighed. "When I was a kid, I never once heard the word *sex* spoken at home. *I* never even said the word until I was in my twenties. It was crazy."

He blinked, gave a short laugh. "Okay." He rubbed the back of his neck, frowning. "Don't know how to respond to that."

Lindsey slumped against the seat, embarrassed and frustrated. "I don't know why I said that out loud."

He caught her chin, brought her gaze back to him. "We pushed some boundaries last night," he said quietly. "It's probably normal for you to be thinking back on things you were raised to consider taboo."

It wasn't fair. Why did he have to be gorgeous *and* understanding?

"You're having regrets, aren't you?" he said, weaving his hand through her hair.

She thought about it for a second. "No, I'm not." She gazed deeply into his eyes and swallowed around the lump in her throat. "You look as if you are, though."

"My only regret would be if I hurt you in any way." His hand slipped around to cup her head, and he drew her toward him. He gave her a chaste kiss on her lips.

"Then—" She almost said "don't," but stopped herself just in time. "Then hurry up and show me your house."

The truth was suddenly crystal clear. She would inevitably end up hurt, but it would be her own damn fault.

RICK CARRIED IN her small flight bag, and she took in the sack with the coffee and box of chocolates. He insisted they go in through the front door and not the carport door that led to the kitchen, which Lindsey thought was kind of cute because she assumed it was about her first impression. But she quickly learned he had a more practical motive. He didn't seem sure about the condition of the house. Had he been the last to leave, he would've known, she reasoned, which took her right back to that stupid dark place in her hapless brain.

He took her bag to the bedroom, presumably inspecting the house along the way. She waited in the living room, which was small, furnished with only a leather couch and a glass table. But the best part of the room was the large plate glass window, where she stared out at the spectacular view of the ocean. In the distance, two sailboats glided through the sparkling blue water. Closer to shore a group of kids bodysurfed. It was pretty incredible, so beautiful and serene.

She glanced over at him when he appeared from the back of the house. "If I lived here, I would never leave this place. This spot."

"My bedroom has the same view." From behind, he circled his arms around her waist, and rested his chin on her shoulder, pressed his cheek to hers. "Want to see the rest of the house, or do you want to make out?"

Lindsey laughed. So did Rick.

She crossed her arms over his and leaned back against his chest. "It's quiet here."

"Occasionally the traffic noise can be annoying, but at night it's pretty cool, you can hear the waves break."

"You lucked out finding this spot." She knew real estate like this was pricey, which made her curious, but not enough to be rude and ask. "Did you have the house built?"

"Nope. It's actually twenty years old, but the previous owners had it totally remodeled."

"Aren't you afraid someone will build in front of you and block your view?"

"I own the land all the way to the highway. The beach is public. So, yeah, I really did luck out."

"What about hurricanes? Isn't it scary to be this close to the water?"

He hugged her tighter, and she could feel his smile against her cheek. "Even paradise isn't perfect, sweetheart. But damn sure worth the risk."

That was one of the many differences between them. Rick wasn't just willing to make changes or take risks, he took the initiative, while she hid in the corner of her safe little life, watching the world go by, content knowing that her future was secure as long as she didn't step over the line. When she thought about it like that, her existence back in Chicago seemed rather sad. All the more reason to be glad she'd thrown in with Mia and Shelby. Taking the risk would probably end up being the best decision she'd ever made.

"Want a tour?" he asked. "Only two bedrooms, two bathrooms, a closet-size office and the kitchen. Won't take long. Then we'll hit the beach."

"Oh, great." She glanced down at the pale contrast of her arms against his. "I'm so ridiculously white maybe I'll get lucky and blend into the sand."

He leaned away to look at her, an eyebrow cocked in amusement. "Blend in? No way. You're one of a kind. Come on."

She smiled in spite of herself, then let him take her by the hand to the back of the house. He hadn't been kidding about the place being small. Though the master bedroom was large with that killer view of the ocean, and the adjoining bath had a big ol' whirlpool she had every intention of sinking into. But the other bedroom was smaller, hosting a double bed, no headboard, no nightstand. A brass lamp sat on a cardboard box.

The tiny office surprised her. Unlike the sparsely furnished rest of the house, a desk, two computers, and wall-to-wall shelves crammed with books crowded the room. Oddly, it wasn't messy, just sort of overflowing. In fact, the house was impressively neat and clean. She wondered if the woman he'd chased out had done his housekeeping.

No, not allowed. She wasn't going to go there and spoil the rest of her week. With some effort she replaced the doubts with white noise, and preceded him to the kitchen.

The incredibly state-of-the-art kitchen.

"Whoa." She stopped abruptly in the doorway, jolted into taking a step when Rick ran into her. "This is amazing."

"Yes, and no, I don't cook."

"Then why?" She swept an arm toward the stainless steel appliances, not the inexpensive models, but the subzero, convection brands that serious cooks dreamed of owning once they won the lottery. There was a large butcher-block island, lots of gleaming black-and-white tile and gray granite.

"This is the way the house came. Boosted the price, but that's okay. I'll get it back and more on resale."

"You're thinking of selling?"

"Not right now, but that could change."

For whatever reason, that he could even consider selling shocked her. "This place suits you," she said. "Yeah, I mean the house certainly, but this whole area, with the beaches and laid-back lifestyle…"

"For now it does." He shrugged. "Look at you, moving from Chicago to New York to start a business. Two years ago did you imagine you'd be taking this step?"

She faked a shudder. "I can't imagine I'm doing it now."

Rick grinned, and gestured toward the back door. "It's good to shake things up. You don't know where you're going to land but it might be a better place."

"Or in an alley somewhere."

"Quite an imagination for an accountant."

Through the window over the sink, she saw something outside, a sunroom maybe, but the way the sun was shining into the window it was hard to tell. "What's out there?"

"Um, it's supposed to be a patio/outdoor living area, or whatever you want to call it."

She could see a fire pit and a massive barbecue island partially sheltered by flowering plumeria trees and lush ferns. "May I go see?"

"I don't know." He peered between two parted blinds with a doubtful frown.

"Sorry." She stepped back. "I didn't mean to be nosy."

"It's not that. Besides my office, that's my favorite place to hang out. The problem is that I'm not sure what kind of condition it's in."

"From the weather?"

He snorted. "A tornado can cause less damage." He let go of the blinds. "Occasionally I let a few of the kids that work at the shop crash here. My office and back there are supposed to be off-limits, but sometimes they get carried away and…" He shook his head, plowing a frustrated hand through his hair.

"The place looks clean," Lindsey remarked.

"Yeah, well, I'm not sure how it looked a few hours ago." He noticed a water ring on the granite countertop and used a dishtowel to rub it off. "Before I left for Waikiki I specifically said no one could crash here until further notice. I didn't want you coming back with me and thinking I was this total slob."

She grinned. How adorable was that?

He opened the refrigerator and offered her a choice between a diet cola and a beer. She took the cola. He got another one out for himself. "Some of the kids around here have pretty bad home lives. I'm not stupid about it, but I do have an open-door policy to a select few. They're generally respectful of my things, and then again I don't keep much stuff around. But sometimes other kids follow them over here and things get out of hand. I've only had to call the cops twice."

Her brows shot up. "Only?"

"That's in four years. Trust me, with the kind of crap that goes on with some of these kids, that's not bad."

"Opening up your home like that is incredibly nice of you," she said, meaning it. She didn't think she could be that generous with her personal space.

"What am I supposed to do when a kid has no place else to go? They can only sleep on the beach for so long." An apologetic smile chased the concern from his face. "Hey, enough about that, how about we go to the beach now?"

"Or we could clean up the patio if need be. I don't mind helping."

"I know you wouldn't." He touched a finger to her lips. "We have too little time together. I'm not wasting any of it, especially on cleaning. Besides, I've got the kids who sometimes do it."

Lindsey's thoughts shot back to the store parking lot, and she stared at him, registering reality in measures. "That phone call earlier, I thought—" She clamped her mouth shut, quickly turned away and snapped open her can of cola.

"You thought what?"

"Nothing. I—I overheard something I shouldn't have."

Rick moved around the butcher-block island and cut her off. "You want a glass?" he asked, studying her face.

"No, thanks." She forced herself to meet his probing eyes.

"What did you think, Lindsey? You were obviously upset at the shop."

"It was really stupid, okay? Can we please drop it?" Her cheeks had to be redder than a cherry tomato.

He said nothing for a horribly long five seconds, and then asked, "You have your swimsuit on under that?"

She nodded, sighed quietly with relief.

"Then let's go surfin'."

"Oh, God, I hope that was a figure of speech."

Rick chuckled, looped an arm around her neck, kissed her mouth hard. He reared his head back and smiled at her. "I'm going to show you why there is no place on earth like the North Shore."

LINDSEY THOUGHT Rick would grab his board while she picked up a couple of beach towels, and they'd run across the highway. Wrong. According to him, the waves weren't big enough. So he strapped his board to the top of the Jeep and they drove a few miles to Sunset Beach.

As soon as they turned off the highway and she saw the waves, her stomach nearly leaped into her throat. They were huge, nothing she'd ever seen before, especially with people out there, some on boards, some flailing around. Rick, on the other hand, was disappointed. He gauged the waves at eight feet. He'd been hoping for ten-foot sets.

They got out of the Jeep, but Rick didn't unload his board. He leaned back on the hood, his arms folded, and from behind dark glasses, he stared out at the waves. Lindsey's breath caught just looking at him. All bronzed and chiseled, he looked as if he should be on a magazine cover.

Two guys heading toward the water with surfboards under their arms yelled something to him about Waimea. He nodded, made some kind of hand sign she didn't understand.

"Are you really going into the water?" she asked, a bit nervous for him.

He smiled at her. "I don't have to. I can stay here on the beach with you."

"But if I weren't here, would you be surfing?"

He caught her hand and pulled her closer. From his pocket he withdrew a tube of sunscreen. "Probably."

"You know I can't go in there, right?"

"I wouldn't let you."

She raised her brows in reproach.

"Excuse me. I meant to say that I would highly

discourage you from going in with waves this high."
He tried to hide a smile while he unscrewed the cap.
"We should have put this on back at the house. Take off
your top."

"Does that line usually work?"

"You'd be surprised." He squirted the white cream
into his palm.

Lindsey blinked at his insensitive response. That
wasn't like him. He probably hadn't been thinking. He
had seemed a bit preoccupied since they'd left the house.
"I don't know...I might leave my shirt on."

"You want that kind of tan line?"

"No, I guess not." She pulled up the hem of her tank
top, then peeled down her shorts and threw them both
into the Jeep. She glanced down. The bronzing lotion
she'd now used twice had helped some but not enough.
"I think I might be the whitest human being on this side
of the island."

Rick took her by the shoulders and turned her around.
He rubbed the sunscreen down her back, and whispered
into her ear, "You look terrific." He slathered the cream
across the back of her thighs. "Good enough to eat," he
added, trailing the tip of his tongue inside her ear.

"Stop it," she said, laughing and trying to pull away.
"You know that tickles."

He banded his arms around her, kept her rooted to
the spot.

She gasped, glanced around to check for an audience.
"You have no shame."

"None," he agreed.

"Rick, you know these people. I don't."

"That's right. So don't worry about it." He turned

her around and leisurely kissed her, before refilling his palm and rubbing the sunscreen on her chest. Although he was discreet, he wasn't shy about reaching into the bikini cups and making sure her skin was covered with the cream.

When he swept his palm across her ribs, she sucked in her stomach and shivered a little. Everything tightened—her nipples, between her legs…

He smiled, as if he knew exactly what he was doing to her. She couldn't see his eyes behind the dark lenses, and maybe that was for the best.

"I can get my legs after I sit down. Let me do your back," she said, half expecting him to balk.

He squirted more of the sunscreen into his hand, and then gave her the tube and his back while he rubbed the cream into his face and chest.

"I didn't know you could wear sunscreen and get this tan." She massaged his shoulders and back, loving the feel of his bunching muscle under her palm, and staring at the four-inch tattoo, a Hawaiian symbol he'd gotten in memory of a friend, a fellow surfer. She glanced nervously at the waves.

"I spend a lot of time in the sun."

"Do you ever work at the shop?"

"I have a back room where I'm playing with a new board design." He turned to face her. "Which isn't public knowledge, by the way."

She nodded. "How is that coming?"

He shrugged. "Let's go find a spot." He grabbed the towels and tossed them over his shoulder.

"I'll take those. You've got your board to carry."

He unloosened the strap. "I figured you'd take it for me."

Her eyes widened on the surfboard. It had to be six or seven feet long, who knew how heavy. "I'll try."

Rick lifted the board and sent it nose-first into the sand in front of her. "Here you go." By his beginning smirk she knew this was some kind of test or joke.

She gingerly took hold, careful to keep it balanced, and then jerked her head up. "It's light. It's like... foam."

"Yep." Grinning, he took the board from her. "Everyone expects them to be heavier than they are. The old ones were made of wood. Those suckers were heavy."

"Dude, where you been?" A man—early twenties, his dark hair and brown skin dripping wet—approached them. He planted the point of his board in the sand. "I figured the shoulder had you taking it easy and drowning in six-packs."

"No way." Rick greeted him with one of those weird handshakes that made Lindsey think of sign language.

"You missed it this morning, dude. Sets of twelve-footers, amazing." With the back of his wrist, he wiped the moisture from his face and eyed Lindsey.

"I'd introduce you, Pono," Rick said, sliding an arm around Lindsey, "except you're a dog, and she's off-limits."

The man laughed, his dark brows shooting up in surprise. "Ha, dude, must be serious." He picked up his board. "Later," he said, winking at Lindsey as he headed toward a group of parked cars.

13

"WHAT WAS THAT?"

"What?" Rick tucked his board under his arm, with his free hand he caught Lindsey's and started them toward the sand.

She glanced over her shoulder. "I guess it's a subculture I don't understand," she said diplomatically.

"Because you thought I was rude, or because I got all caveman on you?"

"There is that."

Rick kept an eye on a young surfer riding a seven-foot funboard who was about to wipe out at any second. "Pono's a nice enough guy, but the minute I would've left you alone, he'd have been all over you."

She blushed. "Don't worry about me. I know karate."

He slanted her a long look. "Seriously?"

"No." She grinned. "But I like surprising you once in a while."

"No worries in that department." He shook his head, pausing to watch as Ryan paddled out. The boy was too green. He had no business being in the white water. "Damn kid's not using a leash," he muttered to himself.

"Excuse me?"

He glanced at Lindsey. "Sorry. I see someone out there who should still be using the kiddie pool. How about here?" he asked, halfway between the grass and the water.

"Sure." She laid out the beach towels, while he put down his board.

Rick didn't sit with her. He waited until he could make out who was manning the lifeguard station. It was Brian. Good man. The lifeguard waved when he spotted him, and Rick signaled for him to keep an eye on Ryan.

"You guys sure are big on hand signs," Lindsey said teasingly when he sat beside her. "Is it universal surfer speak or do you have to be a private member of the club?"

"A few are universal, used mostly if a guy cuts you off. I think you'd recognize those," he said, chuckling as he crouched beside her. "The lifeguard's a friend of mine. I asked him to watch out for one of the kids. If it seemed cryptic it's because I don't want to embarrass the boy, though I just might kick his ass in private." Rick sighed when he saw Ryan make a bonehead move, and glanced at Lindsey. "Figuratively speaking."

She was smiling at him, a weird pleased smile like the kind his sister sometimes gave him when he was playing with his nephews. It made him uneasy. "It's nice that you care that much," Lindsey said.

He shrugged. "The local surfers out here are a good bunch. We try to help each other out." He stood, stretched out his legs, his arms. "Mind if I go out for a few minutes?"

"I forgot about your shoulder until Pono brought it up. Are you sure it's okay?"

"Fine."

Her anxious gaze swept over the swells. "Those are awfully big waves." She looked up at him, her blue eyes fretful, doing the talking for her. She wanted him to be careful. She wished he wouldn't go out there at all because she was afraid for him.

He broke eye contact and picked up his board. He didn't need that kind of concern. Hell, he didn't want Lindsey to care that much. It would only end up bad for her.

"I won't be long. Just need to whisper a few sweet nothings to a couple of hotheads out there." He hesitated, thought about kissing her before he left, but then just headed for the water.

This would be a good test for his shoulder. He hadn't been in the water for over four weeks. The doctor had told him to sit out for six, and as much respect as Rick had for someone who powered through four grueling years of medical school, ultimately he knew his own body better than someone with a certificate hanging on their wall.

The water was cooler than he liked, but still warm considering it was March. It felt good slapping against his thighs as he waded in before hopping on his board. He paddled out to catch up with Ryan and Sam. Neither boy was ready to take on six-foot waves, or Sunset, period. They were too eager, too immature to understand the danger. Both of them knew how many great surfers had drowned out here, but at their age they thought they were infallible.

He understood because it hadn't been that long since he'd similarly regarded life and his future. But that wasn't what was bothering him today. It was Lindsey. So, he liked her. Maybe too much. They had three and a half days left before he'd be driving her to the airport. It was going to be tough saying goodbye. For both of them, he admitted. But he had a feeling it would be worse for her.

Women like her didn't check out a week of their life as if they'd checked out a library book. Use it for seven days, return it on time, no harm, no foul. She'd probably end up analyzing the hell out of everything they'd done and talked about, and then kick herself for putting it all out there. He had a younger sister who used to cry on his shoulder every time she broke up with a guy she'd been serious about. Thankfully, Jenny had been married for three years now.

After he realized Lindsey had overheard his call to Wally about making sure the place was clean, he understood the wrong assumption she'd made. The thing was, at any other given time, it could've been true. He liked women. There were plenty around who liked him, too. No promises were ever made. No one got hurt. They came and went. They didn't gaze at him with concern in their big blue eyes. If anything, they wanted the rush of being with the dude who wasn't afraid of Waimea at thirty or forty feet.

Sometimes the situation went sideways. If a woman got too clingy, he stayed out in the water for hours and tended to clam up until they got the hint. Never his finest moments, but that's the way he was, the way he was built.

Lindsey was different. It was those eyes. If he hurt her, those blue eyes would haunt him forever. He'd see them in the blue depths of the ocean, he'd see them in the blue of a clear sky. Oh, he had a feeling it would be a long time before he stopped picturing that sweet innocent face, the one filled with concern for him. And that would be all on him. Wouldn't that be something?

He saw Ryan paddling toward the big outside sets, and Rick cut loose a string of obscenities that would make a drunk soldier blush. He yelled to get the kid's attention. Ryan couldn't hear him.

Before he could paddle out to the boy, a huge wave rose up and crashed down on Ryan. He was floundering in the white water by the time Rick reached him, meanwhile Rick's shoulder was aching. He totally deserved every ounce of pain. Ryan had been only half the reason Rick had stubbornly paddled out after the first warning twitch. He wanted to show off for Lindsey. What an ass.

He managed to grab Ryan and put him on the front of his board, which was too small, but he had no choice. He paddled outside of the impact zone with Ryan hanging on by his fingernails. Rick glanced back, saw another huge wave rising up on the horizon and hoped like hell that Brian had seen what had happened and was on his way out with the big rescue board.

LINDSEY SHADED HER EYES. The sunglasses helped but the glare off the water made it hard for her to keep track of Rick. She couldn't understand why he'd just kept paddling. The waves had gotten bigger since he went out, at least to her eyes, and she'd started praying that he would turn around and come back to shore.

"Excuse me, ma'am."

She looked up. It was the lifeguard Rick had signaled. He was tall and lean, and keeping his focus on the ocean even while he talked to her.

"Yes?"

"How's Rick's shoulder? Do you know?" It wasn't a polite, icebreaker question. He seemed tense, alert to whatever was happening in the water, and he'd brought a long orange board with him.

"I don't know. He said it was okay." She hadn't realized she'd gotten up on her knees until now. She quickly scrambled to her feet. "Is he in trouble?"

"He's trying to help a kid," he murmured, half to himself. Without tearing his gaze from the waves that seemed to be coming at a more rapid and terrifying pace, he ran with the board into the surf.

Lindsey's heart somersaulted. She strained to locate Rick. The waves were high and when they broke, there was nothing but white spray. Most of the surfers had swum to shore. A few were still out there. The spectators who'd been sunbathing were all standing now and staring out to sea.

Fear tightened in her chest. She couldn't see Rick. She just wanted to be able to see him. Even in her panic, she was furious with the lifeguard. Why had he wasted time asking her about Rick's shoulder?

"He's gonna be okay."

She turned sharply, saw that it was Pono, the guy Rick had spoken to earlier.

"That's nothin' for Rick. I've seen the dude out at Waimea at twenty-five feet."

"Do you see him now?"

Pono pointed vaguely to the right.

Lindsey saw nothing but waves breaking and crashing. "I don't understand why the lifeguard waited so long. He wanted to know about Rick's shoulder instead of going out there and helping him." Her voice was shaky, her whole body had started to shake.

"Brian's helping another dude." Pono touched her arm, got her to look at him. "He asked about his shoulder because he wanted to make sure Rick was okay first."

She turned back to stare at the frightening water. But what if he wasn't okay? Men were stupid about admitting vulnerability. He could be hurting and unable to help himself, or the boy. She shuddered uncontrollably.

"What's your name?"

"Lindsey," she answered grudgingly.

"Look, Lindsey, Rick's the best. No lie. If it was me out there in trouble, he's the one I'd want saving me. The dude is a world-class big-wave surfer. Everybody around here knows that. Even if he won't commit—" He pointed again. "There he is. He's got the kid. Ah, you're kidding, it's Ryan."

Lindsey saw him about twenty feet from the shore and she ran toward him. The boy was lying prone on the board. Rick trudged through water, pushing the surfboard, his chest heaving.

"Is he okay?" Lindsey's gaze darted from the boy to Rick. "Are you?" She stopped when the water slapped her thighs.

The kid lifted his dark head, pushing the long wet hair away from his face. "I lost my fucking board."

Rick tapped the back of his head. "Watch your language."

The boy glanced sideways at Lindsey, and slid off the board with a sullen expression on his face.

"You're lucky that's all you lost." Rick looked tired, he looked as if he might be hurting.

Pono had run up behind Lindsey and took over the surfboard. "Ryan, you dumbass." He smacked the side of the boy's head much harder than Rick had. "What's up, dude? You know better."

"Shut up." Ryan jerked away, his face red with embarrassment.

Walking backward, anxious for them to be on dry land, Lindsey touched Rick's wrist, gazed helplessly into his weary face. He gave her a faint smile and rested his arm heavily around her shoulders. She slid her arm around his waist, her feet sinking deep into the wet sand, the water swirling around her knees.

"Where's Brian?" he asked, craning his neck to see toward the water. "I saw him go in."

"He's paddling in now," Pono said. "Some dude got caught in a break too far outside. I think it was a tourist. Shoulda left 'em." Chuckling, he winked at Lindsey.

She didn't know how everyone could take what had happened so lightly. Her heart was still pounding so hard she was a bit dizzy. Even Rick seemed calm, just tired, and twice she caught a small wince which probably had to do with his sore shoulder.

By the time they reached dry sand, a dozen or more people converged on them. They all talked at once, most of them more impressed with the size of the unexpected waves than anything else.

When the lifeguard came in with the man he'd rescued, a few people wandered over to them, but most of the crowd stayed put. They all seemed to know Rick, and wanted details, and to trade war stories about rogue waves and daring rescues by helicopter.

Lindsey had been elbowed aside in the crush. She didn't mind, and shook her head when Rick tried to draw her back into the circle. If she thought he needed to lean on her, she would've instantly gone back to his side. But listening to everyone chatter was fascinating. Some of the people—mostly teenagers—sounded like fans. They practically worshiped Rick. Not a single person had had a doubt that Rick could have brought the boy in safely.

Ryan had plopped down on the sand, his head hung as he pummeled a piece of driftwood into the ground. Rick was mostly quiet and broke away from the crowd twice, only to be drawn in again. Two gorgeous blonde women wearing thong bikinis were all over him. He obviously knew them, and each pressed him to let her take him home. That was the first time Lindsey had seen Rick blush a little. It made her smile.

"It's over, folks," he said abruptly. "Everyone is all right." He stepped away, glanced over at the lifeguard who was shaking the rescued tourist's hand, and then at Ryan. "I'll see you at the shop, huh?"

The boy nodded, a weak smile softening his brown face before he went back to punishing the sand.

"Rick?"

He turned his head. So did Lindsey. A woman stood off to the side. She had shiny brown sun-streaked hair that hung to her waist, and a stunning bronze body barely covered by a few strips of buttery yellow fabric. Her almond-shaped brown eyes reflected her concern.

"How's the shoulder?"

He shrugged. "Okay."

"You need me, you call," she said softly.

"Thanks, but I got it covered." He smiled at Lindsey, held out an arm to her. "Let's go home."

Feeling a bit awkward, she sidled up to him, and waited until he slid an arm around her shoulders before she slid hers around his waist.

They started toward the Jeep, and she promised herself she wouldn't ask. She kept her word for five whole seconds. "Who is she?"

"That's Lani. We saw each other for a while."

"What happened?" She felt him tense. She knew she had no business being nosy but she didn't retract the question.

"We wanted different things. I'm sorry but I might have to wrap my shoulder when we get to my house."

"Please. Don't be sorry. I knew you were hurting."

He squeezed her shoulders tighter and kissed her hair. "No acrobatics for us tonight."

She blushed. "Shut up or I'll hurt your other side."

Rick grinned. "What happened to my sweet—"

"Your surfboard." She stopped. "And the beach towels—"

"Don't worry. Someone took care of it." He shaded his eyes, squinted toward where the Jeep was parked. "Pono is strapping my board on now."

"Wow. That's really nice."

"Yeah. It's a pretty tight community."

"Is Ryan going to be okay?" she asked, frowning after him.

"So you worry about everyone, not just me, huh?"

She sighed. "Sad to say, that's partly true. But you—" she lightly jabbed a finger in his chest "—don't ever do that again."

"What? I shoulda let Ryan drown?" he said, his brow cocked in amusement.

"Would he have?" she asked, renewed fear tightening her chest.

"Don't go there. It'll eat at you." He opened the passenger door. "Let's go home."

She nodded, hating that she loved the way that sounded.

14

THE NEXT AFTERNOON Lindsey cleaned up the kitchen after making them an early dinner. At her insistence, they'd hung around the house all day, talking, reading the news on the computer and then he taught her to play chess and she whipped his butt at Scrabble. There had been kissing, too. Lots and lots of kissing, but they'd been careful about doing anything else.

Although Rick wouldn't admit it, his shoulder was still bothering him. Lindsey knew because he'd had a rough night trying to get comfortable. She'd practically begged him to go get an X-ray after the incident yesterday, but he was a stubborn, grouchy patient. She was beginning to think his pride hurt as much as his shoulder.

Lindsey hadn't hounded him since late morning so when she heard him grunt, she decided to give it one more shot. "Are you sure you shouldn't go to the doctor?" She set their drinks down on the glass table next to him, a beer for him, wine for her.

"Say that one more time, Linds." His voice carried a very definite warning. "Just one more…"

"Or what?" She grinned as she sat beside him on the couch, curling her legs beneath her.

At her dismissive tone, his brows lifted and he grabbed her wrist. "I'll tear off your clothes and make love to you in ways you've never dreamed possible."

She laughed, but the sound came out funny when she nervously swallowed at the same time. He looked positively yummy sitting there with his hair still damp from his shower, wearing unsnapped jeans, no shirt, his bare feet propped up on the brown leather ottoman that matched the couch.

Outside the large glass window the sky was cloudless, a perfect match to the sparkling blue ocean, yet his hazel eyes seemed more green today.

She pried his fingers from her wrist, and his hand dropped on her thigh. He slid his palm up a few inches, burrowing his fingers under the hem of her shorts. "You're not allowed to move around," she reminded him. "Furthermore, I'm not sure a beer is smart. What if you end up having to take a painkiller?"

"One lousy beer. Please. And I already told you, I don't take painkillers."

"Testy, aren't we?"

"Not testy. I'm horny."

That startled a laugh out of her. But she didn't blush. Another surprise. "You can't be."

"Yeah?" He glanced down at his lap.

Her gaze followed to the straining zipper of his jeans. Her pulse quickened. "Not advisable," she said weakly.

He gave her a tolerant smile. "There are a lot of things we could do that won't hurt my shoulder."

She blinked, moistened her lips. This time the blush came with a vengeance.

"All the kissing. You looking the way you do...what did you expect?"

She tugged at her sloppy ponytail. "Looking the way I do? Very funny."

"You're beautiful, Lindsey." He lightly squeezed her thigh and, using his elbow for support, leaned over to kiss her. He fell short by a couple of inches. "Move closer."

"I don't want to hurt you."

He smiled. "Then come here."

With mock annoyance, she scooted her butt closer to him, her mind racing ahead to the luscious things he would do to her.

He shoved his hand under her T-shirt and cupped her breast through her bra. "Why did you wear this?"

"My bra?"

"You knew we were staying in." He unfastened the front clasp, pushed the cup aside and fingered her nipple.

"I always wear one," she muttered, irritated with her banality, but turned on, too.

"Take it off, but leave the shirt on."

She frowned, but did the magic trick she'd learned the first day she was forced to change in a locker room. In seconds she laid the bra on the couch and waited.

He smoothed the T-shirt over her breasts, and stared at her nipples poking at the soft fabric, his expression one of pleasure and an odd fascination. Lowering his head, he dampened the material in both spots with his tongue and then leaned back to inspect his handiwork.

"Your version of a wet T-shirt contest?" she asked in a breathy voice.

"No contest. You win hands down." He leaned back in and blew lightly on the damp material clinging to her hard nipples.

The feel of his warm breath on her covered breasts did amazing things to her entire body. She put her hand on his chest, let it slide down to the waistband of his jeans.

"First your shorts," he whispered.

She understood immediately and swung her feet to the floor. The blinds were open but the reflective glass prevented anyone from looking inside. Lifting her butt, she got rid of her shorts.

"Your panties," he said, his eyes hooded and watchful.

Without hesitation, she slid them off, her thoughts flashing back to the first time he'd asked her to undress. She'd been too shy. Amazingly, that was only days ago. How could something that felt so major happen in such a short time?

Her T-shirt wasn't nearly long enough to hide everything, and as she curled into a safer position, she considered with some amusement that she hadn't exactly been reborn.

Rick smiled, as if he knew what she was thinking. He reached under her shirt again, kneaded each breast and teased her nipples. "Let me use my mouth on you," he murmured in a low husky voice, and then trailed his splayed fingers down her front, stopping to urge her thighs apart. "I want to make you come."

She automatically tensed. "But you'll hurt your shoulder."

He smiled, kissed her chin. "I don't plan on using it."

The inevitable blush warmed her skin. So did his unbelievably deft and soothing hand, working its magic and melting her resistance.

"It's okay," he said. "No pressure."

"No." She swallowed hard. "I want you to."

"I know it's a very intimate thing. Not something I practice freely," he said, and she frowned. "You don't believe me."

"I do. I mean…really?" The idea was more a curiosity to her than anything else.

"Really."

"How many times have you done it? Less than five?"

"Lindsey," he said, his tone part rebuke, part amazement, his small smile infinitely patient.

"Sorry, I uh—" She clamped her mouth shut, possibly more embarrassed than she'd ever been in her whole life.

He laughed, gingerly twisted around on the couch and slid his hand up her thigh. "Lie back."

She hadn't yet gotten over her gaffe, and for her, the mood had decidedly mellowed. Her gaze shifted to his fly. Clearly, he didn't share that problem. The knowledge renewed her excitement. "Will you take off your jeans?"

"I might need some help." He slowly unzipped his fly, careful of the snug fit over his arousal.

Lindsey got up and tugged his jeans down his hips.

Then stared at his extended hand. "It'll be easier in bed," he said, and she helped pull him to his feet.

He held her hand and led her into the bedroom. Her heart raced, knowing what was about to happen. She only wished she didn't feel so awkward, and when he told her to sit at the edge of the bed, she didn't protest or even bother to think, she simply obeyed.

"Lie back," he told her, urging her down with two gentle hands at her shoulders.

It was a scary, vulnerable feeling to have her feet on the floor, him spreading her legs as she reclined.

"Relax," he whispered as he lowered himself.

"That can't be comfortable—"

"Shh." He crouched between her legs, stroked her with his hand before entering her with his finger.

She went limp and closed her eyes. The tingling started low in her belly, just like it always did, traveling along her nerve endings, into her chest, out to her arms. He took his time, leisurely circling her clit with his thumb. With his other hand, he pushed her shirt up, touched her breast. She shivered with longing, the familiar ache already starting to build inside her.

He put his mouth between her legs. She jerked, opened her eyes. She stared at the top of his head, his long hair brushing her belly, falling on her thighs. As with his thumb and finger, he was in no hurry. His tongue laved and dipped, his moist breath making her hot and cold at the same time. Her head fell back and her lids tightened until all she saw were pricks of light piercing the darkness.

Her body began to tense up, but it wasn't because she was nervous. It was the way he licked and sucked at her clit, the way his fingers pushed into her. When he flicked at her with his tongue pointed and hard, she grabbed the covers and gasped.

Without warning she started to convulse. The speed was so startling, the spasms so intense, she tried to push his head away from her, but he stayed with her, the urgency of his mouth feeding her sensual panic until she had no fight left in her. She went limp again, breathing hard.

Rick stretched himself out, pressed his mouth over hers. She sampled herself on his lips, the unfamiliar taste oddly erotic. He felt a bit heavy with only his good shoulder to lessen his weight.

"I think you set a record," he murmured, chuckling against her mouth.

"Holy shit," she murmured back.

He lifted his head, and stared at her in total astonishment.

She covered her mouth with her hand, muttering a muffled, "I've never said that before in my life."

Rick laughed, really laughed, then grimaced when he bumped his shoulder on her knee.

"Get up." She carefully shoved at his chest. "Come up here." She scrambled away from the edge, and pulled him up by his good arm.

"Wait," he said. "Stop. It's better if I do this." He sprawled out beside her, managing to grab her T-shirt and yanking it up.

"You faker."

"I'm not. It hurts, but I want that shirt off."

She didn't hesitate getting rid of it, and sat facing him

without a stitch on. Her pale skin had blotched, but he didn't seem to mind, or notice.

He reached out and touched her breast. "Get a condom," he told her, adding, "Please," when she made no move.

She swallowed back the last bit of nervousness. "Not yet. I have my own plans." She used the tip of her finger to touch the silky crown of his penis, and then bent her head and followed the same path with her tongue.

He hissed in a breath. "You don't have to do this."

Moisture had formed at the tip and she lapped at it, swirling her tongue as she'd seen him do to her breasts. Feeling brave, she took as much of him into her mouth as she could, startled at his jerk when her teeth scraped him.

She straightened. "Did I hurt you?"

"No." The tenderness in his smile made her heart flutter. The rest of her melted. "Seriously, Linds. You need to get a condom."

This time she did as he asked, then passed him the packet, afraid her hands would tremble.

He quickly tore it open, sheathed himself. Mindless of his shoulder, he caught her hips and urged her to straddle him. She readily sank onto him, unprepared for the depth of the penetration. She clenched around him, then just started to move when he threw back his head and cried out her name.

THE NEXT DAY Rick swore to her that his shoulder was better and they had lunch at a cute outdoor café that specialized in locally grown food. He'd warned Lindsey that he needed to swing by the shop afterward, and any place they went that kept him out of the water was fine with her.

While he was in the back going over paperwork with Wally, she looked through the racks of women's T-shirts, tank tops and shorts. Rick had suggested that she pick out whatever she wanted, and because she'd run out of clean clothes she decided to take him up on the offer. Basically she needed only one outfit to get her back to Waikiki since she would be leaving Hawaii the day after tomorrow.

The depressing thought churned bitterly in her stomach. Darn it, she couldn't go there. It wasn't fair, not to Mia and Shelby, who were counting on her to return to New York, her batteries recharged and ready to tackle the new business. It wasn't fair to Rick, either. The only thing he'd signed up for was a week of no-strings fun.

And as for herself, this was supposed to be a week of renewal, saying goodbye to the old her, hello to a braver, more interesting Lindsey Shaw. Not a sniveling crybaby who'd fallen so hard for Rick that she could barely think about that inevitable last time they'd make love, that final glimpse of him as she boarded a plane knowing she'd never see him again.

They could promise to talk from time to time, and they probably would, but that would fade over the months and wouldn't prolonged contact be more painful anyway?

Nope, she wasn't gonna think about it. She gave her head a shake. She wanted to be stronger and braver. Better she start this minute or totally ruin her last day with him. She noticed some posters on the wall, large stills of giant waves. She moved closer and saw they were photographs of surfers who looked like small toy figures against the monster waves that had to be over thirty feet high. Why anyone would put themselves at risk like that was totally mind-blowing.

Lost in thought, she hadn't heard the voices behind her. She glanced over her shoulder and saw two teenage boys. When he saw that she noticed them, the taller one gave her a cocky grin and strutted toward her.

"Can I help you with something?" He had to be about sixteen, but he had a deep voice, slightly accented with a local inflection she was beginning to recognize.

"Do you work here?" she asked.

"Yep."

"Oh, well—"

The other boy stepped up and shouldered the first one, his big dark eyes instantly familiar to her. "Dude, better chill. That's the boss's lady."

She smiled. "Hi, Ryan."

He jerked his chin by way of greeting.

Wisely, she refrained from asking how he was doing in front of his friend. "You work here, too?" she asked him.

Ryan nodded. "I'm a shaper." When the other kid gave him a dry look, he added defensively, "Boss is teaching me."

She had no idea what being a shaper meant but it sounded like an important job judging by the pride in his voice. "I'm Lindsey," she said to the other boy.

"I'm Kai." He boldly sized her up. "You live here?"

"I'm visiting."

"Just the young man I wanted to see." Rick's voice came from the back of the store, making Ryan cringe.

He muttered a curse under his breath, darted a brief, pleading look at Lindsey, then hung his head and shuffled in his rubber flip-flops toward the back.

"Lindsey, I'll only be a few minutes," Rick called out.

She started to tell him to take his time then realized Ryan wouldn't appreciate that. Uncomfortable under Kai's intense scrutiny, she turned back to the posters.

"Ever seen him surf?" Kai asked, his dark piercing gaze swinging from her to one of the posters.

"Who?" she asked.

"Boss," he said impatiently, his gaze narrowing as if he didn't trust her. Odd because he'd been flirty at first.

She focused on the poster, moving in closer. Her gaze zeroed in on Rick's name in black letters in the corner, then widened on the man partly crouched on the surfboard, an enormous wall of water curling over him.

"That was Waimea at thirty." It was Wally's voice behind her. "Kai, you have work to do outside in the shed."

Lindsey slowly turned around, vaguely aware of Kai's long parting look as he wove his way around the racks to the door.

"Don't mind him," Wally said. "He doesn't understand why Rick won't go pro anymore. Sees everything and everyone as an obstacle."

She frowned. "Pro surfing?"

Wally grinned. "Not a fan, huh?"

She gave a sheepish shrug, her attention inexorably going back to the poster. "I mean, I knew Rick surfed, although…did he tell you what happened the other day?"

"Yes, ma'am." He stroked his wiry beard. "He's chewing Ryan out now. The boy will think twice before taking on those kinds of sets again. I guarantee you that." He fixed his gaze on the poster. "The kids all listen to Rick. They know he gives a damn about them, makes sure they go to school, gives them jobs. That's the only reason he has this shop." Wally chuckled. "It ain't because he makes any money at it."

Lindsey remembered something Pono said about Rick being a world-class surfer. At the time she'd been too frightened for his safety to give the remark any thought. "And that's why he didn't stay a pro?"

Wally gave a noncommittal shrug. "He won a lot of big prize money, but he never committed to the sport. If you wanna be recognized, you gotta travel, you gotta surf full-time, accept endorsements. The big sponsors, they all want him." He shrugged again. "Can't treat it like a hobby. It's all about commitment, plain and simple."

She lifted her chin. "Well, you'll probably hate me for saying this, but I'm glad he's not serious about it." Her gaze went back to the poster. He looked beautiful, graceful, an athlete's body. Easy to understand why sponsors wanted him. "It's too dangerous," she murmured. "In fact, I wish he'd never get on another surfboard again."

"That's different." Wally was looking at her with a strange expression.

She blushed. "Not that it's any of my business."

He laughed heartily at that. "Don't think that'll happen, him not ever surfing again, but I figure he'll move on to the next thing soon enough. He doesn't have the right drive. Rick doesn't live for that next big wave."

"Is that so terrible?"

"Not to me. Not to you." His faint smile nearly hidden by his bushy beard, he added, "It is to the kids around here, to big names who want him to wear their logo. Lots of pressure."

It apparently mattered to a lot of women, too, she'd noticed. At the beach, at restaurants. Not that she blamed them. "Rick doesn't strike me as someone who caves in to demands," she said more indignantly than she'd intended, and glanced sheepishly toward the back. She had a lot of nerve discussing Rick, but she couldn't resist one more question. "Why tell me all this?"

"Because you're somebody who matters to him." Wally's amused gaze swept her startled face, as he ran his hands over his ribs, much like a man who had just finished a satisfying meal. "And vice versa, seems to me. Guess it's time for me to get back to work." He turned away with a smile.

"I'm leaving the day after tomorrow."

"Then you have a nice trip." He said with an over-the-head wave and no backward glance.

She stared after him, then at the poster, her heart doing double time. He was wrong. Rick clearly hadn't shared their unspoken deal, for which she was grateful.

"Ready?" Rick's nearness made her start. He glanced at her empty hands. "You didn't find anything?"

She shrugged helplessly, not trusting her voice. Too much was swirling around in her head. From what she'd seen and from what Rick had told her himself, he and

Wally were close. So what did the man know that she
didn't? He'd claimed she mattered to Rick. She had no
reason not to believe him. Oh, how much she hoped it
were true. Rick made her feel special and she knew he
cared, but enough to make it work for them once she
left for New York?

He smiled, pulled her into his arms. "You'll have to
shop later. We need to go home."

"Why?" she asked breathlessly.

He nuzzled her neck. "So I can talk you into staying
an extra week." He kissed her surprised mouth, murmuring against it, "And to get my way…I'm not gonna play
fair."

15

RICK HADN'T LIED. HE hadn't played fair. Not even the teeniest bit. He'd had her stripped naked and close to begging for release within an hour of them crossing the threshold. The adorable creep had even played the pity card, pretending that with his injured shoulder he'd be helpless without her.

As if she'd needed convincing. But she hadn't given in all the way. He'd pushed hard for her to stay a week, but she'd stood firm, agreeing to two extra days. It killed her to make the compromise, but she had Mia and Shelby and their new business to consider. Though her friends had been great about everything, even urging her to take whatever time she needed.

Lindsey still felt a little guilty, but there was something happening here in the North Shore, something she had the feeling was a turning point. A risk she was willing to take.

What had totally impressed her was Rick's organizational skills. He'd immediately set a plan in motion, making the roundtrip to Waikiki to pick up the rest of her luggage and making a list of must-see sights to maximize her remaining time. When she reminded him to check out of his suite, he'd already done it. Over breakfast he'd asked her about their new concierge/rental business, and gave her some great ideas they hadn't considered. She'd teased him about the engineer in him showing, and he'd made a face, then quickly changed the subject.

There were so many things she wanted to ask him—about his professional future, about surfing, about how long he thought he'd stay in Hawaii, all touchy topics with the potential of ruining their last days together. So she stayed silent.

The day she originally was supposed to have left, they hiked to Waimea Falls and had a picnic lunch, then stopped at Waimea Bay. Everywhere they went people knew Rick. Whether it was at the small market where he shopped, at a restaurant or one of any number of beaches. It was crazy. Kind of overwhelming, sometimes annoying. Especially when other women acted as if she weren't even there.

At the bay, people were surfing, but the waves weren't big, according to Rick, anyway, not for Waimea. They had to be at least seven feet, enough for Lindsey to clench her teeth. She was almost glad his shoulder still ached if it meant keeping him out of the water. When he suggested they stay in the Jeep and watch, she was all for it. Maybe she'd actually have him to herself.

"What do those bumper stickers mean?" she asked, indicating the pair of small SUVs parked side by side, each displaying the same sticker that read…Eddie Would Go. "You have some T-shirts in your store with that saying."

Rick nodded. "It's a reference to Eddie Aikau, a local legend. He was an award-winning big-wave surfer and the first lifeguard hired to police the North Shore back in the seventies. In all his years as a lifeguard, the guy never lost a single person here at Waimea Bay. And we're talking thirty-foot waves or more at times. Other lifeguards wouldn't go in during certain conditions, but not Eddie. Wish I'd known him."

"He's—" She couldn't say the word. All she could think about was the terrifying day at Sunset Beach when Rick had gone after Ryan.

Rick narrowed his gaze on her. "He's dead, but it wasn't a surfing accident, if that's what you're thinking. I doubt you've ever heard of the Hokule'a." She shook her head. "It was the name of a double-hulled voyaging canoe built by a local group who wanted to duplicate the voyage the ancient Hawaiians were thought to have taken between Hawaii and Tahiti.

"This was back in the late seventies, apparently it got a lot of press at the time. The trip was almost three thousand miles. Eddie volunteered to be one of the crew members." Rick shrugged. "One of the hulls sprung a leak, the canoe capsized. Eddie had taken his ten-foot gun with him—" Rick stopped, smiled. "That's a surfboard. Anyway, he started paddling toward Lanai to get help. That's the last time anyone saw him. Ironically, the rest of the crew was rescued."

"Oh, my God, that's so sad."

"Yep. People here took it really hard. I know a couple of veteran surfers who used to lifeguard with him. They swear he was every bit as awesome as the stories say, a great role model to the kids at the time."

"Kind of like you."

He snorted, regarded her as if she'd been smoking something funny. "Not even close."

She slipped an arm through his. "How many kids do you have working at your shop?"

"I don't know. Maybe a dozen. Why?"

She smiled. "How many do you actually need?"

He lifted a brow. "Keep it up and I'll do things to you that'll make you turn three shades of purple."

"Promises, promises." She let out a yelp when he stuck his hand up her shirt. "Stop it." Laughing, fighting his plundering hand, she glanced around. "Go ahead, try and distract me, but I know things. Like how you always buy bread for Aunty Leialoha to feed the birds and pretend Jimmy is the one who saved her the stale loaves."

"Oh, what a horrible secret you know about me." He unclasped her bra.

"Hey." She grabbed his wrist, and smugly added, "Auntie Leialoha knows, too. She's the one who told me."

Frowning, Rick stopped his roving hand. "No way."

"Sorry, busted. You're one of the good guys and everyone knows it." She grinned when he rolled his eyes. "You're going to be a good father."

Everything inside of her froze. Appalled at what she'd said, she had to concentrate on the simple act of closing her mouth. But it was an innocent remark, she told herself as she watched his jaw tighten. "Obviously I don't know if you're even planning on having kids…I was only making an observation.…" she said, her voice trailing off.

Why one earth hadn't she left it alone? Did he think she was fishing? Should she assure him that she wasn't looking to extend their relationship beyond the next two days? It would all be over soon. The sex. The intimacy. The teasing and laughter. Waking up next to him.

The truth hurt. Really hurt. Far more than she would've dreamed possible two weeks ago when she'd been sitting at her desk in windy Chicago wondering if she'd see him again. And then there was that short conversation with Wally at the shop. She had to admit that since then she'd been thinking more about the possibility of a future with Rick.

"I'll probably have kids," he said quietly, staring out at the waves. "Some day."

She didn't respond. Only stared at him. She figured she'd done enough damage, though he didn't sound put off. But it would be so typical of him to say something—anything—strictly to put her at ease.

She cleared her throat. "Me, too, I guess. I haven't given it much thought yet."

He did her the favor of keeping his gaze straight ahead, though she thought she saw the corner of his mouth hitch up a bit. After a stretch of silence, he said, "If I had a daughter, I'd be strict."

Lindsey stared at him then. "What?"

He gave her a fleeting smile. "I would. Not crazy strict, but I'd set firm boundaries."

"Wait, what about if you had a son?"

"I'd be…" He chuckled. "Probably not so strict."

"Wow. I didn't think you'd be sexist."

"Hey." Rick snorted. "That's crap."

"You don't see raising a daughter differently than a son as a double standard?"

"Okay, maybe. But your parents were strict with you, and look how well you turned out."

Lindsey gaped at him. "There's strict, and then there's puritanical. It's not easy to develop a healthy attitude toward sex with overzealously protective parents."

"I see your point, but it's not gender-related."

"Why are we having this stupid discussion about kids, anyway?" she muttered irritably, then immediately felt badly. Though he was responsible for her being tired and grouchy. She hadn't gotten a full night's sleep since she arrived.

"Tell you what," he said, turning the key in the ignition. "Let's go home and work on that healthy attitude."

IT WAS GOING TO BE a bitch after she left tomorrow. Rick walked out of the master bathroom with a towel wrapped around his waist, and just stared at her. Naked under the sheets that stopped at her hips, she was lying on her stomach, her face turned away, partially covered by her long blond hair.

God, he wanted to kiss her awake, but that would be cruel. She'd had too little sleep and would have to face a long plane ride tomorrow. The thought of her leaving hit him hard. The house was going to seem empty as hell, and way too quiet. He smiled wondering if Lindsey knew how noisy she was in the kitchen. She loved all the modern appliances and was terrific at whipping up a meal out of nothing, but she sure liked to bang those pots around.

Damn, he had to convince her to stay a few more days. Totally selfish of him but too bad. She had the rest of her life to be with her friends and work on the new business. Why was it wrong to want to keep her here a while longer? Maybe she could even stay long enough to fly back with him when he went home to Michigan in two weeks.

His mother had a birthday bash planned for him, which he hated, especially since he was closing out a decade in his life, but he'd promised to show up. Lindsey could go with him, meet the folks, then fly on to New York. He'd pay for her to change her ticket again, although he didn't look forward to a rematch over that issue.

She'd been stubborn about paying her own way. He respected and admired her stance, but he had a hell of a lot more disposable income than she had. A few hundred bucks here and there…no sweat for him. But of course she didn't know that, and truthfully, it wouldn't matter to her because she valued her independence.

He still had so many things to tell her. And he would because he trusted her. Trusted that she wouldn't judge him for not conforming to a preplanned life that guaranteed a paycheck every other week. She'd never once pressured him about his future, or about why he wasn't using his engineering degree.

She'd understand that he needed to think and live outside the box if he wanted to be the one who designed the next generation surfboard. He was almost there.…

Uh, he'd told Wally that a year ago.

"I thought I heard the shower," she said, pushing

back her hair and smiling sleepily at him. "What time is it?"

"Too early to get up."

Lindsey grinned, and started to roll over. He stopped her, sat at the edge of the bed and kissed the curve of her ass right above the sheet. He followed the length of her spine, pressing small kisses up her back, smiling when he saw goose bumps.

She sighed. "I can't believe I'm leaving tomorrow."

"Don't go." He felt her tense. "Stay longer."

She hesitated. "I can't. You know I want to, but it wouldn't be fair to Mia and Shelby."

"Have you talked to them lately? They might be busy doing their own thing."

"Not likely. We have a plan. We have a target date to have Anything Goes up and running." She moved away and sat up, her back against the padded headboard, the sheet pulled up to cover her breasts. "We all have a lot riding on this venture."

"I understand. I'm just saying…a few days or a week might not matter. Inventory could have gotten held up, any number of problems could delay the opening. What would it harm to call Mia and Shelby and see what's up?"

Lindsey sighed, a soft patronizing smile lifting her lips, as if he couldn't possibly understand. "I wish I could stay. I really do."

"Got it." Annoyed, he tightened the towel around his waist before he stood. She looked like a damn mother patiently explaining to her child that they couldn't stay at the zoo all day because Mommy had to work.

"Rick, wait."

He stopped, raised his brows in question.

"Please don't be angry."

Yeah, he was pissed, but he didn't want to ruin their last day. He breathed in deeply and forced a smile. "I want you to stay. You can't. I don't like it, but I get it. That's all."

"You said you still go back to the mainland sometimes, right?" She let the question hang in the air, and so did he.

It was his damned bruised ego. He ought to tell her everything right now. About the patent, the money that had been so carefully invested that he could live off the interest alone. But when she asked him what he had accomplished lately, what would he tell her?

He had no right being angry with her. Lindsey wasn't being inflexible out of stubbornness. She needed to have a plan, a steady course in life. It made her feel safe. He knew that about her from the first night they'd met. He was still amazed that she'd stayed two extra days. That right there told him so much about her. But in the end, she needed the security, the routine. Where did that leave them? He needed a playmate, not a partner.

"Why don't you get up," he said, sitting down again. "I'll spare you my lack of culinary skills. We'll go out to breakfast, then take a nap later."

She moved closer, kissed his shoulder. "How does it feel today?"

"Horrible. I'll be an invalid after you leave."

She smiled, her gaze falling to the tattoo. She traced the J with her fingertip. "Who *was* that woman?" she asked with a laugh.

"I don't know," he said, cursing the tightness in his chest. "But I like this one better."

THEY STAYED OUT the entire day, but didn't do much. Lindsey picked up a few boxes of macadamia nut clusters, to which she'd become far too attached, and souvenirs for her parents and a former coworker in Chicago. Then they stopped at the shop so she could say goodbye to Wally. Rick had a couple of the kids who were working the afternoon shift pack up an assortment of In Motion T-shirts, tank tops and visors for her to take back. She knew her brothers would adore the ones with the words *North Shore, Oahu* emblazoned over a gigantic wave.

Unfortunately, just about everything they did was a reminder that she'd be leaving tomorrow, which had made for a very subdued day. By evening, the lump that had lodged in her throat since their earlier talk still hadn't dissolved. Maybe it had been a mistake to stay the two extra days. She didn't know how she could gracefully say goodbye tomorrow.

She'd barely touched her dinner at the quaint waterfront restaurant Rick had chosen, but she drank three glasses of wine. Yep, she was tipsy and all the way home Rick teased her about the things he would do to her, and how he would take full advantage of her condition and convince her to stay.

It was all so sweet and sad, and she didn't know how she was going to get through the night and tomorrow morning without crying. Why she'd thought the wine would help was beyond her, she thought as they parked in the carport.

"You didn't lock it again," she said to him when she got to the kitchen door first.

"I usually do." He came up behind her and steadied her on the second step. "When I'm not distracted."

"I'm not drunk," she said.

He smiled. "I know."

"Just so *you* do." She pushed open the door. "Anything you do to me, I will remember tomorrow."

"I hope so."

She stepped across the threshold and sighed. "I'm gonna miss this kitchen."

"Is that all you're going to miss?" he whispered in her ear, his warm breath skimming the side of her neck. He plucked the bow that held up her sundress.

"Hey," she said, giggling and trying to keep the halter in place.

He took her wrists, held them together with one hand above her head and used his free hand to touch her bared breasts.

"You can't do that," she said, laughing and walking backward down the hall toward the bedroom.

"No?"

"Nope."

"Hmm…" He smiled. "Looks like I am."

She twisted her hands free and pulled up the top. She almost got away, but he caught her around the waist.

They stopped and suddenly looked at each other, as if it hit them at the same time. The bedroom lamp was on. Rick frowned. "Did you—?"

She shook her head.

He shoved her in back of him and quietly approached the bedroom door. Lindsey followed close behind.

"Sorry, Rick. I thought she'd left." It was a woman's voice.

"Godammit, Lani." Rick pushed a hand through his hair, glanced over his shoulder at Lindsey.

She knew he was trying to block her view, but she stepped to the side to see around him. The woman she'd seen at Sunset Beach slipped out of Rick's bed. She was naked.

"How did you get in?" Rick was nervous and angry. "You certainly weren't invited."

"The door was unlocked," she said, shrugging slim shoulders, in no apparent hurry to cover her large breasts. She pulled on a pair of brief shorts, no panties. "I thought you were alone. Figured you might want some company."

Rick turned his back on her and took Lindsey by the shoulders. "Baby, I'm sorry. I don't—I don't know what the hell to say."

Lindsey swallowed. "It's okay. She thought I'd left," she said, her voice sounding too weak.

Lani had pulled on a short snug T-shirt that bared her taut belly, and touted the In Motion logo. She stood at the doorway, waiting for them to let her pass. "I really am sorry," she said to Lindsey, and then as she squeezed by Rick, she whispered, "Call me." She tried to touch his face, but he jerked his head away.

Rick stared angrily after her. Lindsey simply stared at him. She had started to shake, and she was suddenly freezing. Vaguely she wondered if her legs would carry her to the couch.

Even in her semishocked state, she knew Rick was upset and angry and had nothing to do with Lani being here. None of that mattered to Lindsey. She was exhausted and cold and she desperately wished she were already on that plane flying home.

"Wait here, okay?" Rick lifted her chin. "Okay? I'll be right back."

She stared into his tortured face, startled to see fear in his eyes. She'd seen him annoyed, curious, amused, angry, aroused, but she'd never seen him afraid. He waited until she nodded, and after he walked into the guest room, she stared at his bed. The bed where they'd made love countless times. She'd made it this morning, with all the extra pillows. It was rumpled now. Because of Lani...

Oh, God. Lindsey pressed a hand to her stomach. She hoped he didn't think she could sleep in that bed tonight.

Rick was back. He draped a blanket around her shoulders and walked her into the living room. He sat first, then pulled her onto his lap and cradled her to his chest. He kissed her hair. She used to like it when he did that. She shivered uncontrollably. It had to be the wine. He held her tighter.

How could she have been so foolish? She'd overheard the guys on the beach talking trash, she'd seen the women throwing themselves at them. She could only imagine how easy it was for someone like Rick to get whatever he wanted.

For a horrifying second she pictured Lani, then herself before she banished the image from her mind. How could Lindsey have ever thought Rick would be interested in her? Oh, for one week, sure. She was a novelty. But she didn't belong in this crowd that treated sex so casually. She belonged in New York, doing what she'd promised to do.

"Lindsey?" He sounded broken. "I'm sorry, it wasn't supposed to be like this." He kept stroking her hair.

"It's okay," she said in an admirably calm voice. "This isn't your fault. The week is over, and—" She had to stop or risk dissolving into tears.

"Try to sleep," he whispered, and kept holding her, while she tried to deny she'd stupidly fallen in love with him.

16

THEY DROVE IN SILENCE. Lindsey wanted to leave for the airport two hours early, and there wasn't anything Rick could do or say to stop her. After her solitary shower, she'd shared a cup of coffee with him, telling him more about Anything Goes. She seemed excited about the new business. He understood she needed something to focus on, something other than what had happened last night.

Shit, last night. He could barely come to grips with what had happened himself. There was absolutely nothing going on between him and Lani, but that wasn't even the point. He could barely look into Lindsey's eyes. Although he didn't understand why not. For one of the very few times, he didn't know what she was thinking.

By the end of the night she'd seemed calm, and eventually had fallen asleep. He knew because he'd been awake the entire night, the desire for violence simmering inside him a new and menacing feeling. If he hadn't been holding her, he couldn't have trusted himself not to tear down his house with his bare hands.

He saw the Honolulu International Airport exit, and

it took every bit of his willpower not to drive past the damn ramp and take her to the beach where they'd spent their first night. Start the whole damn week over. But a person couldn't go back and rewrite the past, that's why they had to stay on course and do it as well as they could the first time. Lindsey had taught him that six years ago.

Departures was crowded. Lots of tired mopey tourists at the curb, unloading luggage from cabs. He hated this new security bullshit that prevented him from seeing her off at the gate. He found a spot, and squeezed the Jeep in between a tour bus and a green SUV.

A skycap approached them, but Rick waved him off as he climbed out of the Jeep. Lindsey called the man back.

"I'm taking your luggage to the counter for you," Rick said, his jaw clenched.

She shook her head, gave him a sad smile. "We'll say goodbye here. You'll have to move the Jeep, anyway."

"Let them ticket me."

"No." She indicated her bags to the skycap, then turned back to Rick. She wore her sunglasses. He wanted to rip them off. "I had the best time. I'm so glad you saw the post on Facebook."

"Lindsey." He caught her cold hand. "I wish last night had gone differently."

She moved a shoulder in a small shrug. "It still would've brought us to this moment." She went up on tiptoes. "Thank you," she said, and kissed his lips.

He pulled her into his arms, hugged her so tight his shoulder ached like hell. "Call me when you get there, okay?"

She wouldn't answer.

"I just want to know you're safe." He swallowed back a lump of emotion. Lindsey needed to feel safe. She needed a man who could promise her that. Could he? He didn't know....

"Promise me you won't go surfing with your bad shoulder," she whispered, and pulled away from him.

He saw the track of a tear on her cheek below her sunglasses. "Promise." He barely got the word out.

Abruptly she turned and walked briskly toward the sliding terminal doors with the skycap. He wanted to call after her. But he didn't trust his voice.

THE MINUTE LINDSEY landed in Chicago, she texted him. He immediately tried calling back. She couldn't talk to him, not yet. Maybe in a week or two. It had been difficult enough to call Mia from the Honolulu airport and lie to her, even though the lie was one of omission. Lindsey had asked for an extra two days. Mia assumed she'd be staying in Hawaii with Rick. She didn't know Lindsey was stopping over in Chicago so she could have some time to lick her wounds in private.

What irony. She'd adamantly refused taking extra days to be with him, and now she was forced to take them to get over him. Not for one second did she think that would happen in two days. But if she could just take the edge off before seeing Mia and Shelby, whose drive from Houston had delayed her as well.

She splurged on a cab to her old apartment. It was bare, her few furnishings having been sold off, donated or shipped to New York. Technically she had five days left on her lease so she didn't feel like a squatter. She dropped her two bags in the middle of the small living room, then turned up the heat. She'd worn the wrong traveling clothes for her return because she hadn't been thinking clearly. She still wasn't, but at least she was alone. She could cry her eyes out, and not worry about sunglasses, or strong arms wrapped around her....

A sob tore from her throat. She kicked off her shoes and crumpled to the floor next to her flight bag and curled into a fetal position. More sleep would help dull the pain. Thinking about him wouldn't. Nor would beating up on herself. She'd done enough of that on the plane.

The truth was everything had happened exactly as planned. Lindsey had wanted to break from her boring predictable life. She wanted to change, to take risks. Her week in Hawaii was to have been the threshold to her new life. Charge her batteries, make her fearless and ready to tackle Anything Goes. She choked out a snort. Fate was sure having a laugh at her expense.

Because she *had* changed. She was different than she was ten days ago. Definitely stronger. More positive about her future, not so frightened over having left her job. She had no choice. Her friends were counting on her and she'd never let them down. Mia and Shelby were like her family; no, they were her family, much more so than her blood relatives. She absolutely belonged in New York with them, just like Rick belonged in Hawaii with his waves and fans.

She flopped onto her back, dragged the flight bag over for a pillow and allowed herself a small smile. Sometimes even the best plan sucked.

IT HAD BEEN TWO WEEKS since Lindsey had gotten on that plane. Rick had known before she'd left that he would miss her. He simply hadn't known how much. He'd been restless, grouchy, unable to focus. Surfing couldn't hold his interest, nor could work on the new board design. He'd almost looked forward to going home to Michigan, just for the distraction.

Wally had been anxious for him to leave, too. He'd even dropped Rick off at the airport. Then waited until Rick was getting out of Wally's beat-up seventies van before he told Rick to quit being an ass-clown and to call her already.

What Wally didn't know was that Rick had called. Twice. And reached her voice mail. He'd left messages, and she replied by text—very brief, very polite texts. She had asked him about his shoulder. That was something. She'd also told him how much she was enjoying settling into a routine in New York and meeting the challenges of the new business.

Routine. Yep, Lindsey liked her routine. He hoped she was happy.

He surprised his family by arriving a day early. Then further shocked them with a new haircut. It wasn't too short, not like when he was in high school, but a ponytail was out of the question. Everyone was busy with jobs and school until the weekend and he thought about seeing if any of the nearby ski slopes were still open. He found two, then decided he had no interest. He stuck around his parents' house, and played with his nieces and nephews after they came home from school.

The morning of his birthday he slept in. Or tried

to. His sister Jenny walked into his old room, singing "Happy Birthday," in that tuneless voice of hers.

He muttered a curse, and piled another pillow over his head. Which she yanked off. "Hasn't the state passed legislation against that mouth of yours yet," he grumbled, glaring at her through bleary eyes.

"*My* mouth? I hope you're not using that language around my kids—your nieces and nephews."

"Once in front of Bret. By mistake. I apologized."

"I know. He told me. He's old enough to have heard it before." Jenny chuckled. "I never thought you'd take turning thirty so hard. I'm shocked."

"Too bad not shocked speechless." He burrowed his head under the pillow again.

And again, Jenny snatched it. "It's not about the big 3-0. Look at you. Every young lady in the neighborhood is all atwitter that you're home. You're gorgeous, and you've never worried about age." She paused for a long, drawn-out moment. "Is it a woman?"

He sat up, rubbed his face and sighed. "Screw thirty. I'm grumpy from working too much. I think I'll go play with the kids."

THE KIDS WERE supposed to have distracted him. So were his obnoxious brothers, and they managed to do just that for a while. When they called for an arm wrestling rematch, he refused because of his tender shoulder. He knew what that would mean, and let them heap on the crap about being an over-the-hill wuss, until finally their wives made them shut up.

Rick just sat back and smiled. His mother seemed a bit concerned about him, but he pestered her in the kitchen for a half hour, long enough for her to believe everything was normal. The women were cooking for the big dinner. His nieces were playing with the new dollhouses he'd bought them, and his younger nephew seemed to play with anything that made maximum noise.

As unaccustomed as he was to the racket and small squabbles that occasionally broke out, Rick enjoyed watching the kids the most. Funny, how he'd never seriously thought about having a family. These visits home when everyone got together were always his favorite times.

Lindsey had thought he'd make a good father. At the time, she'd kind of rattled him. Man, talking about kids…that wasn't something he thought about. Kids were a huge responsibility. Took needing a plan to a whole new level.

Yet, he was thinking about it now, he realized, his heart beginning to pound as he studied his three-year-old niece, Chelsea, with her pretty blond hair and sky-blue eyes. He pictured himself and Lindsey loving, worrying, protecting a child. *Their* child. Like he did with the kids at the beach, only a hundred, no, a thousand times more. If anything, his surfing life had taught him that kinds need firm but fair parents. Parents who cared no matter what. Lindsey could be all that with one hand tied behind her back, but as for him? He searched his heart and his mind, and the answer was clear. Yeah. He could do that. For a wife, for a family. Holy…he didn't just want kids. He wanted to make babies with Lindsey.

He swallowed and straightened. What would be so

wrong with having the big noisy house just like he grew up in? A big yard where the neighborhood kids could play ball, maybe even big enough to have a pool, too. Lindsey could plant flowers beds if she wanted. He rocked when it came to barbecuing.

Yeah, the house, the kids, he could get down with all of that, he realized, but what he wanted more than anything was Lindsey.

"Hey." Jenny brought him a beer. "You all right? You look pale." Her gaze troubled, she touched his forehead. "You're clammy."

He took a pull of the ice-cold beer, let the brew slide down his dry throat. "You were right. It's about a woman."

Jenny sat beside him, laid her head on his shoulder like she had since she was a kid. "I knew it. I've never seen you like you've been these past two days."

He smiled. "You'd really like Lindsey."

"So when do I get to meet her?"

"I don't know that you ever will."

Jenny got to her feet and glared at him. "She lives in Hawaii?"

"New York."

Her hazel eyes widened. "Good God, what is that—a two-hour plane ride? You have to go. You do."

Rick smiled. "You don't even know what happened between us."

"It doesn't matter. I know you. Go. You have to go."

"Can I wait until after Mom serves my birthday dinner?" he asked teasingly.

Jenny laughed. "Yes, you may. In the meantime, I'll find you a flight."

LINDSEY HEARD THE DOOR open. She noted her place in the ledger on her computer screen and looked up with a smile, expecting a customer. "May I help— Rick?" She closed her mouth, opened it again, but there were no words. Maybe missing him so very much during the endless days and nights had sent her over the edge.

"Hey, Linds." He looked so handsome dressed in a black leather jacket. And his hair... "Good job on advertising. The place was easy to find."

She adjusted the clip she used to keep her hair away from her face but the tickle of a tendril on her ear let her know she'd only made things worse. "What are you doing here?"

"I came for you."

She laughed nervously, only she didn't sound a thing like herself. "What do you mean? It's a bit far to hop over to take me to lunch."

"I didn't come to take you to lunch."

"Oh, it was just a figure of speech." She helplessly glanced over her shoulder. Shelby was in the back room waiting for a delivery, but she could appear at any second. This was crazy. She couldn't stand here talking to Rick like everything was all right. Except it was, wasn't it?

She'd been holding it together really well. Shelby and Mia suspected something was up, but they'd bought that she simply missed Rick and Hawaii and would get over it.

"I miss you, Lindsey," he said quietly, watching her, his intense gaze overlooking nothing. "Something fierce."

"I've missed you, too," she admitted, because it was

the truth, and if she hadn't he'd know she was lying. "You cut your hair."

"Yeah." He shrugged, raked his hand through the back. "Made my mom and sister happy."

"Your birthday. You went to— Was it yesterday?" she asked even though she'd remembered, and had thought about calling him at least fifty times. When he nodded, she came around the counter to give him a hug. "Happy late birthday."

He held her tight and buried his face in her hair. "God, how I've missed you."

She trembled, ordered herself to move away. She only managed to back up a few inches. "It's not enough, you know."

"Missing each other?"

She nodded. "You can't know someone in ten days."

"And eight hours?" He smiled.

"Don't," she said. Because she wasn't strong, not when it came to Rick. Seeing him weakened her resolve, shook her reason and made her ache, but dammit, she'd come so far. "The sex was great. Better than great." She glanced back, lowered her voice. "Honestly, I didn't know it could be that way. But consider what we do know about each other. We're like night and day."

"If I were three years younger, or even two years younger, I'd have to agree. Not now. We aren't that different, Lindsey. You think you don't know me, but I opened myself up to you, more than I've opened myself up to anyone. Even six years ago, I listened to what you had to say. Did you know I finished school because of you? It would've been easy to quit. I didn't need a degree or a job. But you convinced me to stay the course, keep my options open."

"Shelby's in the back," she warned softly.

"Everybody can hear what I have to say as long as *you* hear it. We know each other better than you think, and if I'm wrong, what's the harm in getting to know one another better?"

How could she take such a risk and find nothing? She was already in love with him. He didn't know, and she couldn't tell him. Although, in truth, she was stronger now, more sure of herself. "I'm not Jill," she said finally. "I'm nothing like the woman you thought you knew."

"You're exactly the woman I knew in Hawaii. Did you think you could make yourself over, share what we shared, and me not see you for who you are? Give me some credit." He sighed. "You haven't changed. You've just grown more into the woman you were meant to be."

"I understand, and I agree with part of that, but I'm not Lani, either," she said, immediately sorry she had. She saw how angry that made him, and she didn't blame him because it had come out wrong.

"Do not hold her against me. That is not fair."

"What I meant was that I'm not like your friends, your surfing crowd. I can't treat sex so casually." She darted a look toward the back. Unless Shelby had stepped outside to meet the truck, she'd heard everything. "I need a clear path to follow. I need routine. I need—"

"I know what you need, Linds," Rick said quietly, taking her hand. "That's what's taken me so long to step up. I had to be sure I was a man you could depend on."

Dammit, she was going to cry. She swallowed, wanting to be strong more than ever. "Rick, you—" Her voice broke. She tried again. "You have this great big life and you're not afraid to participate. Me, I'm this little mouse who's content to stay in her small corner. That's who I am."

He shook his head. "My big life? It's all filler, Lindsey. It's just stuff I do until—" He sighed with frustration. "You're right. There is a lot you don't know about me. Things I'd planned on telling you that last night you were in Hawaii. Like how I've done everything in reverse. You think I'm too free with money, don't you?"

Lindsey pressed her lips together.

He smiled. "Yes, I know it seems that way. I made a lot of money when I was twenty, while I was diving I found a fix for this weird pressure valve. I ended up with a patent that made me a bundle. I invested well, and not only do all of my nieces and nephews have college funds, but I don't have to worry for the rest of my life. I've made over a quarter million in surfing prize money, which takes care of the shop and leaves me some cash. If I wanted to commit to the sport, I could make ten times that amount. So it's not about money or commitment, Lindsey." He grinned. "You were worried about the commitment part, admit it."

She blushed. "A little," she said, breathless as so many things fell into place.

"Are you wondering why I never mentioned any of this?"

"I suppose so." It was quite an understatement.

He took a deep breath. "I didn't want to disappoint you."

She frowned. "I don't understand."

He shrugged, the hesitance on his face unnerving. "Ask me anything you'd like. The first thing that pops into your head."

"Rick, I don't know what you want—"

"Take a minute, think about everything I just told you. Then ask me something. Anything."

Lindsey tried to wade through the ocean of information. "Anything, and you promise to tell me the truth."

"Yes."

"How's your shoulder?"

Rick blinked, then started laughing. "That's the only question you have?"

"No, I have another," she admitted, "but I want you to answer that one first."

"The shoulder is good." He flexed it. "Almost perfect."

She eyed him closely. "Have you been in the water?"

He smiled. "No, I have not been in the water."

She sighed and smiled. "I'm proud of you."

Rick scrubbed at his face, emotion burning in his eyes. "*You* would be concerned *only* with my shoulder," he murmured. "Everyone else wants to know what I've done lately. I'd be asking that question, too. I did, in fact. Until it started eating a hole in me." He shook his head. "There's no one who pushes themselves harder. Truth is, sometimes I try too hard."

Lindsey smiled. "I kind of got that impression."

His brows went up. "How?"

"Your office at the house and the sketchings you leave around, how you sometimes space out."

"I never space out when I'm with you."

"Mmm, sometimes, when we'd be sitting quietly, looking out over the water or whenever. Just like I did when I would dream about...."

"Lindsey, I love you."

She gasped. At some level she'd known as soon as she saw him walk through the door, but... "I love you, too," she said weakly. "I knew I was in trouble over two weeks ago."

He hugged her, then held her out to look at her. "Trouble?"

"I can't leave New York. I have obligations here." She shook her head. "Mia and Shelby are my family, and we have a business to run. I want it to succeed."

Rick smiled. "You'll succeed. Look at you. You have the most incredible resolve. You're amazing, you know that?"

She smiled back, then sighed. "A long-distance relationship would be tough. I can't take time off now."

"I wouldn't ask you to. I'll move here."

"Rick..." She touched his face. "Here? You'd hate it. You'd miss Hawaii and surfing—"

"Yeah, I'll miss Hawaii. But we'll still visit. Believe it or not, there is surfing on the mainland. Waves aren't so big." He kissed her. "You'll like that."

"What about the shop and Wally and the kids?"

"Yep, I'll miss them. I'll still see Wally when I visit, and the kids..." He shrugged. "They're kids, they aren't going to stick around forever. In a way, they're like family, too. I want great things for them and I'm glad I'm in a position to help." His expression got serious. "But I want my own family, Linds. Our family. Marry me."

Lindsey's heart swelled. Hadn't she once thought he'd

make a good dad? So why was the fear still there? She loved him. She believed he loved her. "But, Rick—"

He released her, leaned on the counter and smiled that great big smile of confidence she loved and envied. "Bring it on. Throw out every obstacle you want. I'm not going anywhere. I'm sticking around, Linds, until you get it, even if I have to rent a place down the street. I love you. We belong together."

A noise came from the back. They both turned. It was Shelby, her eyes damp. "Lindsey! If you don't marry him, I will."

Even as her eyes filled with tears, Lindsey laughed, then turned back to Rick. "I do love you."

His eyes closed briefly. When he opened them, they were full of love. "For now, that's all I need," he whispered as he kissed her.

Epilogue

Eight months later

"YOU LOOK WORRIED." Lindsey slid an arm around Rick's waist as he studied the new basketball court that had just been finished in time for the community center's grand opening tomorrow afternoon.

"Hmm?" He put an arm around her shoulders, smiled at her upturned face and kissed the tip of her nose. "Nah. I was just thinking I should have put in a third court."

"Good grief. Look how much you've already accomplished in such a short time. We have plenty of room to add another one if we need it later."

He hugged her tighter against his side. "I like it when you say *we*."

"Why wouldn't I? We're in this together, right?"

"Along with Mia and David, and Shelby and Annabelle, not to mention my sister and her brood—have I left anyone out?"

Lindsey drew back to stare at him. Everyone had pitched in, using their respective expertise to make the brand-new center in the middle of a New York City neighborhood a reality. David and Mia handled the legal issues, Shelby the promotion and their friend Annabelle, who worked part-time at Anything Goes, had donated a sizeable amount of money, matching dollar for dollar what Rick had contributed. His nieces and nephews had drawn up the wish list of kids' activities and his sister had helped Lindsey with all the ordering and shipping of material.

Rick had negotiated the purchase price of the gigantic warehouse and then personally designed each detail to maximize the space enabling them to cater to a wide range of ages. With so many people lending a hand, the project had gone quickly and smoothly. But until now, Lindsey had never considered the possibility that they had imposed on Rick's unique dream of providing a safe, productive place for at-risk kids. She wasn't even sure why she felt uneasy now. Something was off with him.

"Why are you looking at me like that?" He frowned at her, his eyes dark with concern. "I know I've been working long hours lately but it won't always be that way."

"No." Lindsey squeezed his arm. "Are you kidding? I love what you're doing with our new brownstone, and this place—" She spread a hand. "You're going to make such a huge difference in so many kids' lives. I just hope we all haven't changed your vision for it too much."

He looked at her with such a surprised expression that she knew that wasn't the problem after all. "These kids nowadays need all the help they can get. If anything, I'm touched that everyone's become so involved." He drew her close, circled his arms around her. "I hate that we haven't had enough alone time."

"I expect you'll make it up to me," she half-teased.

"Yep, we'll have plenty of time alone while we paint our bedroom, the kitchen and the living room."

"That's not what I had in mind." She swatted his butt and he laughed.

"If Annabelle can cover for you at the office so we can go to Hawaii next month, I figured I'd schedule the painters while we're gone."

Lindsey nodded. "She said I could take the whole month if I wanted, but I told her we'd only be gone ten days."

"Hmm, a whole month by ourselves." He kissed the side of her neck, ran his hands down her back until she was flush against him.

"Hey, watch it." She narrowed her gaze when she felt something suspiciously hard in the vicinity of his fly.

"What? No one's around."

"Yeah, but—" She moved her hips. "What is that?"

Chuckling, Rick reached in his pocket. He brought out a small blue velvet jeweler's box.

Lindsey stared while he flipped it open. A diamond solitaire sparkled under the lights. Rick inhaled deeply and then got down on one knee.

"Are you kidding?" she murmured, overwhelmed.

"Lindsey Shaw," he said solemnly. "Finally, finally, will you marry me?"

"Of course I will, you dope. Get up." She tugged at

him until he stood, and she wrapped her arms around his neck while she laughed and cried at the same time.

He lifted her off the floor and swung her in the air. "I love you, baby," he whispered. "I'll always love you."

* * * * *

COMING NEXT MONTH

Available May 31, 2011

#615 REAL MEN WEAR PLAID!
Encounters
Rhonda Nelson

#616 TERMS OF SURRENDER
Uniformly Hot!
Leslie Kelly

#617 RECKLESS PLEASURES
The Pleasure Seekers
Tori Carrington

#618 SHOULD'VE BEEN A COWBOY
Sons of Chance
Vicki Lewis Thompson

#619 HOT TO THE TOUCH
Checking E-Males
Isabel Sharpe

#620 MINE UNTIL MORNING
24 Hours: Blackout
Samantha Hunter

HBCNM0511

REQUEST YOUR FREE BOOKS!
2 FREE NOVELS PLUS 2 FREE GIFTS!

red-hot reads!

Harlequin® Blaze™ brings you
New York Times *and* USA TODAY *bestselling author*
Vicki Lewis Thompson with three new steamy titles
from the bestselling miniseries SONS OF CHANCE

Chance isn't just the last name of these rugged
Wyoming cowboys—it's their motto, too!

Read on for a sneak peek at the first title,
SHOULD'VE BEEN A COWBOY

Available June 2011 only from Harlequin® Blaze™.

"THANKS FOR NOT TURNING ON THE LIGHTS," Tyler said. "I'm a mess."

"Not in my book." Even in low light, Alex had a good view of her yellow shirt plastered to her body. It was all he could do not to reach for her, mud and all. But the next move needed to be hers, not his.

She slicked her wet hair back and squeezed some water out of the ends as she glanced upward. "I like the sound of the rain on a tin roof."

"Me, too."

She met his gaze briefly and looked away. "Where's the sink?"

"At the far end, beyond the last stall."

Tyler's running shoes squished as she walked down the aisle between the rows of stalls. She glanced sideways at Alex. "So how much of a cowboy are you these days? Do you ride the range and stuff?"

"I ride." He liked being able to say that. "Why?"

"Just wondered. Last summer, you were still a city boy. You even told me you weren't the cowboy type, but you're...different now."

He wasn't sure if that was a good thing or a bad thing. Maybe she preferred city boys to cowboys. "How am I different?"

"Well, you dress differently, and your hair's a little longer. Your face seems a little more chiseled, but maybe that's because of your hair. Also, there's something else, something harder to define, an attitude…"

"Are you saying I have an attitude?"

"Not in a bad way. It's more like a quiet confidence."

He was flattered, but still he had to laugh. "I just admitted a while ago that I have all kinds of doubts about this event tomorrow. That doesn't seem like quiet confidence to me."

"This isn't about your job, it's about…your…" She took a deep breath. "It's about your sex appeal, okay? I have no business talking about it, because it will only make me want to do things I shouldn't do." She started toward the end of the barn. "Now, where's that sink? We need to get cleaned up and go back to the house. Dinner is probably ready, and I—"

He spun her around and pulled her into his arms, mud and all. "Let's do those things." Then he kissed her, knowing that she would kiss him back, knowing that this time he would take that kiss where he wanted it to go. And she would let him.

Follow Tyler and Alex's wild adventures in
SHOULD'VE BEEN A COWBOY
Available June 2011 only from Harlequin® Blaze™
wherever books are sold.

HBEXP0611

Harlequin® *Blaze*™

red-hot reads

Do you need a cowboy fix?

NEW YORK TIMES BESTSELLING AUTHOR

Vicki Lewis Thompson

RETURNS WITH HER SIZZLING TRILOGY...

Sons of Chance

Chance isn't just the last name of these rugged
Wyoming cowboys—it's their motto, too!

Take a chance...on a Chance!

Saddle up with:
SHOULD'VE BEEN A COWBOY (June)
COWBOY UP (July)
COWBOYS LIKE US (August)

**Available from Harlequin® Blaze™
wherever books are sold.**

www.eHarlequin.com

HB79622